TWELVE DAYS
With The EARL

ALSO BY SYDNEY JANE BAILY

The RAKES ON THE RUN Series
Last Dance in London
Pursued in Paris
Banished to Brighton
Gretna Green by Sunset

The DIAMONDS OF THE FIRST WATER Series
Clarity
Purity
Adam
Radiance
Brilliance

The RARE CONFECTIONERY Series
The Duchess of Chocolate
The Toffee Heiress
My Lady Marzipan

The DEFIANT HEARTS Series
An Improper Situation
An Irresistible Temptation
An Inescapable Attraction
An Inconceivable Deception
An Intriguing Proposition
An Impassioned Redemption

The BEASTLY LORDS Series
Lord Despair
Lord Anguish
Lord Vile
Lord Darkness
Lord Misery
Lord Wrath
Lord Corsair
Eleanor

TWELVE DAYS
With The EARL

SYDNEY JANE BAILY

cat whisker press
Massachusetts

First Paperback Edition
ISBN: 978-1-957421-97-1

Published by Cat Whisker Press

Cover: Dar Albert, Wicked Smart Designs

Book Design: Cat Whisker Studio
Editor: Chloe Bearuski

DEDICATION

To Beryl Jean Baily

Love you more, Mom!

A NOTE FROM THE AUTHOR

D ear Reader,

In England, they do not call a *sleigh* by that word. They called it a *sledge*, or in some instances a *sled*. I decided not to introduce an Americanism to the story, and so my hero is driving a two-horse sledge.

As for the twelve days of Christmas, or the Twelvetide, the first day started the day *after* Christmas on Boxing Day, when servants were given the day off and, if lucky, a box of goodies. A peculiarity, which confounded my heroine when she was a child, is that Twelfth Night—when they had gatherings and balls and also removed the last of the greenery to avoid bad luck—comes *before* the twelfth day, January 6th.

Why? Because once it grew dark it was considered nighttime, a new night, and therefore, after the eleventh day came the twelfth night, which was followed at sunrise by the twelfth day. And the twelfth day led naturally into the thirteenth night, which no one celebrates then or now.

The lyrics to the song *The Twelve Days of Christmas* have gone through a number of variations. I chose to adhere to the earliest rendition from 1780, as written anonymously in a pamphlet called *Mirth Without Mischief.* The song was listed as having been "sung at King Pepin's Ball."

The only King Pepin whom I can find lived a thousand years earlier, and I wonder if we really know what was sung at his ball. I know I wasn't invited. By the way, Pepin was the father of the famous Charlemagne and also called Pepin the Short, King Pepin I, and Pepin III (because there were two other Pepin ancestors, although neither were kings).

As always, happy reading,
Sydney Jane Baily

CHAPTER ONE

Ramsden Heath, England, 1835

"**R**oast me like the devil's herring! Not you!"

It was a mean-spirited thing to say, not to mention rude to swear in front of her, especially on Christmas eve. However, Lady Patience St. Claire wasn't surprised by the Earl of Beaumont's crass words.

After all, she had insulted him more than once by word and by deed, although never with such common language.

At that moment, his lordship was holding open her carriage door, which was behaving like a hatch in a ceiling since her vehicle had overturned. Luckily, on this frigid December day, thick snow as well as the blankets with which she was traveling had cushioned her.

Still, Patience felt rather like a pea in a rattle. When the door lifted open, she expected to see her driver peering down at her, not her nearest neighbor and year-long foe, Lord Nathaniel Beaumont.

"Are you going to continue gawking at me, given my dire predicament?" she demanded. "Or are you going to assist me out of this carriage? I could have been killed!"

Such an outcome might have been preferable to requiring and receiving help from this particular nobleman. In truth, she did not believe that for an instant. At twenty-two, Patience was more than happy to think she had many years of life ahead of her.

Simply *not* in this man's company. Not with her skirts practically tossed over her head as she sat in a heap, swathed in fur-trimmed wool, with her thick stockings showing above her boots.

Lord Beaumont shot her a wide grin. It was crooked, the only thing not perfect about the man's appearance. That annoyed her further.

"Why are you smiling like a fool?" she asked, managing to stand and sort out her skirts.

"I was imagining closing this door and riding away. You'd be trapped for the Twelvetide."

"You wouldn't!" she said. "I might starve. Or freeze."

"You might," he agreed all too cheerily. "But you won't. By the by, are you injured? Did you receive a blow to the head when you tipped over? Or a broken bone or anything of that nature?"

That sobered her. "No. I am unharmed. The carriage tipped slowly as we rounded the bend. What caused it?"

"Reach up," he ordered while holding his hands down to her.

She did as he instructed, but when he heaved her up by her arms, she yelped. Twice.

"Stop that caterwauling," the earl said, sounding irritated. "Climb the seat and try to gain a higher purchase."

Patience did, but to no avail.

"It's the blasted angle," he said. "Your driver put two wheels on an icy embankment and over you went. Here now, stand to the side as much as possible."

Lord Beaumont's head disappeared from view, making her heart pound. Maybe he was abandoning her to the cold after all.

After he spoke to someone out of sight, a moment later his polished Hessians appeared, followed by tan, wool trousers that were anchored in place by the straps fastened under the soles of his winter boots. She had never seen stirrup straps from such a position before.

Her gaze followed the slight flare of his trousers until they hit his knee where they snugly conformed to his muscular thighs. Patience tried to look away but could not.

The earl dangled in mid-air before dropping into her carriage, at which point his winter coat swooped behind him and concealed his shapely legs from her view.

"*Oh!*" she exclaimed, not because she had lost sight of his well-developed thighs but because *her* front was nearly touching *his* front, without any way to put distance between them. Craning her neck, she looked up at him.

They hadn't been this close since the ball a year prior when he had tried to worm his way into her good graces for the sake of getting his paws upon her estate. With great good fortune, she had evaded him.

Before discovering his motive, Patience had been thrilled when Lord Beaumont, handsome and single, had maneuvered her into an alcove at Lady Kepelton's Twelvetide country house party. After a day of flirtation, he had kissed her soundly, sweetly, and seductively. In the gathering dusk, the perfect kiss had set her heart to pounding and her body humming like a well-tuned harpsichord.

The following day, he had stayed as near as bread to butter. That evening, between dinner and supper, more kisses as well as an intriguing conversation had ensued.

A few minutes later, however, Lady Priscilla Malcolm Price had taken her aside.

"I can see you are taken with Lord Beaumont."

Patience had narrowed her eyes. "On the contrary, I believe *he* is taken with *me*." She wasn't going to let this young woman, a debutante of earlier that season, make her sound eager. *How positively vulgar!*

"Be that as it may," Lady Priscilla continued, "I wish to offer a word of advice as we ladies must stick together. Please be cautious. I heard him speaking with Lady Kepelton about wishing to expand his estate, and how convenient that yours bordered his. All he needed was a quick wooing and an even quicker wedding. Or words to that effect."

Patience's heart had sunk into the pit of her stomach, which had become as queasy as a green sailor. It stood to reason she would make such a misstep at her first country party without her mother by her side. And the earl probably knew of her vulnerable state as an orphan. Everyone in the *ton* had heard how Lord and Lady St. Claire perished when their sailing vessel capsized during a fierce gale.

Regardless, she had lifted her chin and shrugged.

"Beaumont is nothing to me, nor I, to him. Thus, your advice is misplaced."

The next time the earl had approached her, she'd given him the cut direct, turning her back on him in Lady Kepelton's great room, and not letting him get her alone again for the duration of the Twelvetide. Not close at all, nor had she allowed him to sit beside her at any of the subsequent meals.

Patience had departed the house party after the Twelfth Night ball, never to see him again.

She should have known Lord Beaumont was an opportunist. After all, he hadn't bothered to call upon her and pay his respects when her parents had passed away eight months before the Christmas gathering. However, after the spine-tingling kiss that had sent trembling quakes down to her toes and back again, he had sent flowers, a smoked ham, fine fur-lined gloves, and various friendly notes.

Once, he'd even shown up at her door, and she had refused him entrance, making sure he was sent away before he could see too much of the deteriorating conditions of St. Claire Hall.

But she wasn't stupid. Naturally, she'd kept all his gifts.

Today, in the pale light of the gray winter sky, the earl's eyes were a stunning green, and his thick hair was as dark and tempting to touch as ever. She fisted her fingers at her sides.

"Where is your hat?" Patience asked, wondering at a man going without one in this weather.

He frowned. "I'm sorry if my undressed appearance bothers your delicate sensibilities, my lady, but I thought it best to leave my chapeau topside. Do not faint over the indecorous act."

"Don't be ridiculous," she snapped, wishing his fragrant cologne wasn't reminding her of their kiss a year earlier. Still, she took a deep sniff of it—spicey, woodsy, and invigorating. "How does it help for you to be stuck in here, too, breathing all the air and crowding me?"

Patience was certainly warmer now that Lord Beaumont was there. His tall, muscular physique was covered by an overcoat and scarf, and both were touching parts of her coat. It was practically indecent!

He glowered at her, and she returned the stare. Finally, he sighed.

"Easier to lift you from this vantage, my lady, as long as you haven't been indulging in extra helpings of pudding."

"How dare you!" And then his hands were on her person, so she closed her mouth with a gasp, although another "How dare you" would not have been out of order.

"Are you ready?" he called up to the opening.

"Yes, milord." It was her driver, Mr. Crawford. Truth be told, he was also the only male servant she had left, and not a trained driver at all, but she wasn't going to tell Lord Beaumont such a thing.

With his strong hands on her waist, the earl said, "Raise your arms again, my lady."

She did so, glad her cloak concealed the way her breasts rose, too. Yet she couldn't conceal from herself how she felt when his lordship lifted her against his body and then boosted her as high as he could. Patience wanted to wrap her arms around him, relax into his warmth, and be kissed.

Mr. Crawford, who'd once been her footman, was in his twenties and strong as an ox. Thus, he grabbed hold of her wrists and drew her skyward.

It was most uncomfortable. But she forgot the pain when Lord Beaumont's hands continued to assist her passage, by roaming down her body and pushing her up. His palms cupped her rear and then stroked down her legs until he grasped her calves for the last push.

She was out and sitting on the side of the coach with Mr. Crawford's arms around her middle from behind.

"My apologies, my lady," he said helping her stand.

"For what?"

"Touching you," he said, tugging his hat.

"You saved me, and I am grateful."

"I saved you," the earl called out.

Ignoring him, she let Mr. Crawford assist her in descending from the overturned carriage. Ultimately, she slid down the sideways driver's seat to the snow-covered ground.

"I've unhooked the horses," Mr. Crawford added unnecessarily, "while Lord Beaumont was climbing in." Then he said once more, "My apologies."

"For what now?" she asked.

"For tipping your coach in the first place."

"That's all right. You weren't hired as a driver, after all." She was glad he stayed in her service with the meager wages she could afford. Fortunately, he was sweet on her only remaining chamber maid, Eliza, so both stayed on, and everyone was happy. Poor and hungry but happy.

"Hello," boomed the earl's voice. "A little help here."

"My apologies," Mr. Crawford said for the third time before scrambling back up onto the carriage and thrusting an arm inside for the earl to grab ahold of.

Soon, Lord Beaumont was on the snow beside her.

"You should have switched over to a sledge," he advised, "given these conditions." Picking his hat off a snow bank, he hit it against his thigh and replaced it on his thick head of hair.

Such beautiful, dark hair. Patience longed to touch it. But his advice, which sounded rather like a reprimand, annoyed the longing right out of her. She wasn't a ninny, but she'd been forced to sell the sledge months earlier. After all, it was no good most of the year whereas her coach was nearly always acceptable transport.

Except for the past few weeks. *Such a bother!*

All she said was, "Next time."

"Next time what?" he asked.

"A sledge, of course."

He nodded, then pointed at her overturned vehicle. "We cannot right it. Thus, you'll have to ride with me."

Rearing back, Patience shook her head. "Oh, no, no, no, no. If I turn up at Lady Kepelton's with *you*, in *your* sledge, without a maid or companion," she trailed off at the notion of her utter ruin.

The earl laughed heartlessly. "Two things, my lady. One, you would have seemed more than a tad on the shady side arriving anywhere without a maid. Where is yours, by the way?"

"At home in bed." It wasn't a lie.

"Sick with fever?" he asked, concerned.

Why had he jumped to that conclusion? "No. Eliza slipped on the ice at the back door and twisted her ankle." Also, not a lie.

"Then why didn't you bring another one?"

"I have a friend and her mother waiting for me at Lady Kepelton's. They will act as chaperone and companion." A whopping great lie.

"Alas, they won't," he said.

"Whyever not?"

"That's the second thing I was going to tell you. There is no party. It has been called off."

Her heart started to beat harder. Patience had been looking forward to the food and the blazing hearth and to more food. She had a master plan to leave early with her two bags stuffed full of nourishing ham, turkey, potatoes and whatever else she could acquire from her hostess's cook whose great aunt was Patience's own aged cook.

Glancing at Mr. Crawford, she saw the stark terror of starvation cross his features. They had left the two remaining staff at St. Claire Hall with barely enough sustenance for two days. Just bread and broth, turnips and leeks. And since one was his ladylove, Eliza, this new development was none to welcome. The other was their cook, who had nothing left in the larder or pantry with which to ply her trade but stayed because she was as old as Methusaleh.

"I can't see going nowhere else, milady, and starving there when I can do that at home in me own kitchen."

"Sweet mother," Patience exclaimed, wanting to collapse onto the snow rather than return home empty-handed. Maybe she would never get up again.

"Why has the party been canceled?"

But Lord Beaumont was not looking at her, or he might have noticed her frightened visage. Instead, he spoke to her driver.

"Unfasten your lady's trunks and bags, and load them on." He gestured to his spacious sledge, painted a pretty dragonfly green, reminding her of his eyes. Fixed to it were two long runners, polished and gleaming.

"Plenty of room," he added. "But we must be off. There's another snowstorm coming."

Before she could think properly, Patience was ensconced on the seat beside the earl, who was driving himself. They were covered in blankets and cozy as lambs in the manger.

"What about my driver?" she asked.

"My good man," Lord Beaumont said as Mr. Crawford packed the rear compartment with her two nearly empty bags. "I advise you to ride one horse and lead the other. You may come with us or go back to St. Claire Hall."

Then his lordship looked at her. "Your choice, of course, my lady."

In turn, she looked at Mr. Crawford. "Your choice," she muttered.

"I will return home, milady," he said, "to look after . . . things."

Patience knew he wanted to take care of Eliza and her injured ankle.

"Very well. But what about the carriage?"

"Like your skinny horses, it's a bit dilapidated," the earl remarked. "Why don't you abandon it here. Scavengers will take it for scrap."

"Oh, no!" she exclaimed. Being without a coach would be disastrous, leaving her without a civilized way to take long journeys or to gather supplies.

"If you must keep it," Lord Beaumont said, "then your driver can return with a few of your footmen and a groom or two and right the blasted thing."

Patience's mind searched frantically for a way not to lose her only transport.

"Could you send a few of *your* men to bring it safely to *your* home, my lord? I've recently lost my wheelwright, so have no way to get it repaired."

The earl sighed. "No able-bodied maid, no one who can fix a carriage wheel. What kind of place are you running over there at St. Claire Hall?"

However, he didn't really want a response, for he quickly added, "As soon as we reach my home, I'll send someone back for the heap."

"Why don't you simply take me to *my* home?" she asked. "And then deliver my carriage there after it's fixed?"

He paused and caught her gaze. His jade-colored eyes made him look like the Lord of Misrule if ever she'd seen one.

"While I may appear as your humble servant, Lady Patience, I am not. You spent the first few months of this year rejecting my every advance after rudely rumping me, may I remind you, in front of our mutual neighbors and friends and even some of my visiting family at Lady Kepelton's."

Her mouth opened and closed. Should she mention that she knew he wanted her estate? But he was on a rant, barely stopping for a breath.

"So while I find your rear to be fetching, my lady, and don't mind helping to heft it out of your carriage nor have it perched on my sledge seat, that doesn't mean I have forgiven you. I have done you a kindness, I'm doing you another, but the third one is beyond the pale."

Her rear! Lord Beaumont thought it fetching. Patience shouldn't care a whit what he thought of her, but she was pleased albeit shocked that he had spoken of it aloud.

"Besides," the earl finished, "we are closer to my residence than to yours, and it's Christmas eve. We can spend it in one another's polite company since we were both going to a party that has been cancelled due to a nasty smallpox outbreak."

She gasped at Lady Kepelton's misfortune.

"It is not her ladyship, mind you, who is afflicted. Not yet," he added. "Some of her staff who were recently at her London home have fallen ill. She's headed north to her sister's residence in Chelmsford and may God keep her safe. In any case, we might as well make the most of a bad situation, mightn't we?"

Punctuating his words, snow began to fall in thick, moist flakes.

With that, he flicked the reins and his team of two horses began to trot.

Patience could hardly credit that she was seated beside the Earl of Beaumont—all six strikingly handsome, masculine feet of him—and speeding toward Beaumont Manor.

She could only imagine the food!

CHAPTER TWO

Nathaniel couldn't believe his luck. The very female he'd been thinking of was handed to him on a silver platter. A rolled carriage had yielded the fiery-haired Lady Patience, who had snubbed his advances a year earlier, confounding him when he'd thought they were well on their way to an understanding.

True, the understanding might have been based on nothing more than him fancying her pretty face, burnished red locks, and shapely figure, but he had been in a settling-down sort of mood at Lady Kepelton's last Twelvetide party. The intense attraction had him thinking of courting Lady Patience with an eye toward marriage.

However, it wasn't his bruised ego that had caused him to think of her recently. It was the fact that so many of her staff had made their way to his servants' entrance seeking employment.

For a while, he'd assumed she was a hard taskmaster, the kind of employer a servant left at first opportunity. Glancing over at her heart-shaped face and delphinium-colored eyes, he could now safely say he still fancied her.

What's more, he had come to understand that her staff had left because she was mired in unpaid debt.

Family debt. Crushing debt. The kind that made people do strange and erratic things. If she were a man, she would probably be in a London gambling hall trying to reverse her bleak fortunes. As a woman, she could be selling herself along with her estate on the matrimonial market. She was certainly attractive enough to catch a wealthy man.

"Why are you still living alone in your parents' home?" he asked.

She startled. "You are a churl, and a nosy one at that. You should mind your own business."

He laughed.

"I know what you want," she added.

It was his turn to startle because at that moment, he wanted her. Naked, heavy-lidded, her lips parted, whispering his name, and then crying it out when he satisfied her.

"Do you?" he asked, his voice a little raspy.

She shrugged and looked in the opposite direction, toward the barren Essex countryside. "You shall not get it. I live in my own home because it is just that—*my* home. Where would you suggest I live?"

"Sell it and remove the burden. Then you can live in Town." All at once, he had a vague memory of seeing her when they were children, her red hair in braids, when he, his sister, and his parents were in residence at their country estate.

"I came to St. Claire Hall years ago, didn't I? At least once."

"You did," she agreed. "You were a disgusting boy, with your nose in the air because you knew you were the future earl, and you liked earthworms and skinning fish."

He laughed again. "I resent the remark about my nose. I don't recall keeping it in the air, but I know I dug in the dirt for worms and enjoyed casting my line. I still do. Fishing is relaxing. I'll teach you."

Why had he said that? They could not fish in December.

"Anyway, I'm sorry about your parents. Quite a blow."

There were those crystalline, blue eyes, captivating him again. He had to look away as he guided the horses around the turn with a gentle tug on the left rein. Nathaniel ought to have paid her a visit when she was in mourning, but it had seemed forward of him. Nevertheless, he had been happy to see her at Lady Kepelton's a year ago after she'd emerged from her bereavement.

"And I am sorry about your father," she offered.

"Thank you." The previous Lord Beaumont had been more devil-may-care than Nathaniel, a strange twist on father-son relations, in which he had urged his sire to be more prudent. A steeplechase, highly wagered upon, had driven his father to reckless actions, leaving his mother a Dowager Countess and making Nathaniel an earl decades before he'd expected to be one.

"You have a sister," Lady Patience added.

"Yes. Lady Lillian Reynolds. Two years older and happily married, expecting her second child any day."

"A Christmas baby," his red-haired companion exclaimed. "How wonderful!"

Before they could have further discourse, he drove onto the smooth snow of his own drive.

"Beaumont Manor is larger than I remember," she remarked.

Hm. "I didn't know you had ever been here."

"Twice, but you weren't in residence. I think you must have been at university. Your parents hosted my family. After all, we are neighbors."

He felt even worse for not visiting her after Lord and Lady St. Claire died. To his defense, he'd been on the Continent when it happened, and then in London afterward. By the time he'd come back to Ramsden Heath for a month's country respite, dropping in to see her had seemed unnecessary. Maybe considered presumptuous since they were not well known to one another.

Climbing out of the sledge, he turned to help her down. She hesitated, but eventually put her hands out until they rested upon his shoulders. With his hands at her waist, for the second time in less than an hour, he plucked her from the platform and stepped back to set her feet upon the snow.

Deliberately and slowly. After all, she was beautiful and he was a man, and thus, he allowed her body to slide down the front of him.

"You may release me now," she said.

Nathaniel liked holding her, enjoyed seeing her eyes up close and marveled at the perfect pinkness of her full lips. Kissing them had been the highlight of Lady Kepelton's party last year.

"Are you staring at my freckles?" Lady Patience demanded. "I cannot help them. They come with my hair coloring."

He hadn't noticed them. "Your cheeks are ruddy from the cold, but I believe, now that you mention them, I can see a dusting of gold. I don't think anyone would stare at you because of them, however. Why would they?"

"You still have not released me. Moreover, I think most people do not much care for freckles. They are fine on a child, but I am—"

"No child," he finished, feeling her warm curves pressed against him. "I don't think they mar your beauty at all. Personally, I am convinced they enhance it."

Her blush deepened. Apparently, he had embarrassed her with a compliment or two. If only she hadn't drawn him in last year, been welcoming and plainly interested in his overtures.

If only she hadn't returned his kiss like a passionate, red-headed goddess!

Afterward, he had been painfully hard and hopeful the entire evening, believing a country party assignation was in his immediate future, and perhaps something much more.

Why, if she hadn't coolly shunned him a few hours later, he could well imagine they would be married by now. Maybe expecting their own child.

Sighing, Nathaniel released her. It was just as well he did and right on time. Members of his staff had noticed their all-but silent arrival, gliding to the front of his home on the sledge's sharpened and oiled runners. The manor door was already open, and a footman strode out to greet them.

Reaching into the back of the sledge, Nathaniel lifted out her bags. Puzzled, he couldn't help remarking on them.

"They are light as feathers. Where are your trunks full of fancy gowns and dancing slippers for a Twelvetide party?"

He handed both bags to the lingering footman while his head groom led the horses and sledge away. Then he offered her his arm.

"Well?" he asked, still awaiting an answer.

"I wasn't going to stay for Lady Kepelton's entire party."

"Really? And why is that?"

Lady Patience didn't answer, but instead fixed her gaze upon the entrance to his home.

"I still cannot believe you live in such a grand place, practically a castle."

"Scarcely that." Nathaniel's ancestors had remodeled the manor more than once. One section had turrets and a walkway with parapets. And when more space was desired, entire wings had been added in a higgledy-piggledy way.

"If it were a castle, it would be deemed a small one, as far as those things go," he said modestly, though he loved Beaumont Manor and thought it a jewel amongst houses.

"I pretended there were knights here and damsels," she confessed, "when I visited."

Their boots crunched on the frozen ground as they walked toward his portico and the front steps. "What about ogres?"

"Are there any?" she asked.

He looked to see who awaited them at the massive open door, letting all the chilly air inside.

"You might want to watch out for my housekeeper, Mrs. Corely. She can be fierce if you put your boot-clad feet on the furniture. Yet at the moment, my butler welcomes us, and he's a kind soul although a bit of a dolt for holding the door wide."

They hurried inside, and when Lady Patience stamped her feet on his entrance rug, Nathaniel released her arm.

"Mr. Barnes, this is Lady Patience St. Claire. Her carriage overturned nearby."

"We have met before," his butler said when she smiled at him and nodded in greeting.

"Ah yes, the visits whilst I was at university." Nathaniel almost wished he'd been there instead of engaging in waggish and chuckle-headed preoccupations with his friends at Oxford.

"I cannot believe you recall my previous times here," Lady Patience said admiringly. "What a quick and sure mind you have."

"Thank you," Mr. Barnes said quietly.

If Nathaniel wasn't mistaken, his butler's ears were reddening. Personally, he didn't know what all the fuss was about. How could anyone forget a woman with such a crown of ruby hair and glorious indigo eyes?

"Your bags have been whisked inside through another door," Nathaniel told her. That was his assumption, anyway. "They await you in the . . . ," he trailed off, looking at Mr. Barnes.

"Her ladyship shall be most comfortable in the blue room."

"To match her eyes," Nathaniel added before he could stop himself.

His butler didn't alter his expression of utter placidity. "If you say so, my lord."

Lady Patience, on the other hand, looked at him as if he had spoken foolishly. Nathaniel supposed saying such a thing in front of his butler had been a misstep. He was simply excited to have her there. What had nearly been a solitary Twelvetide might prove to be something quite different.

"Would you like to go to your room now?" Nathaniel offered. "And rest after your adventure? Or perhaps have a cup of hot and sustaining tea in my drawing room? Or saloop, perhaps?"

She straightened her shoulders, unfastened her cloak, and handed it to Mr. Barnes, revealing a long-sleeved, lapis-blue day dress. Nathaniel thought the color made her hair appear an even richer, coppery red.

"I should like to greet the rest of your family over a cup of tea. To go upstairs before doing so would be rude."

Nathaniel froze. His butler froze. They eyed one another, two men realizing the female in their midst wasn't going to like what she was about to hear. Not one whit.

They remained silent while Lady Patience tugged off her gloves, a singularly sensual act that stole Nathaniel's breath, regardless of the awkward situation. In fact, he held a large lungful, as he considered how to tell her.

The lady approached the hall's great mirror and started to untie her thick woolen bonnet, which she then placed on the sideboard with her gloves. The only sound was the soft ticking of the seven-foot high, ornately carved longcase clock to the left of the staircase, echoing in the foyer.

"Although, perhaps I should tidy up before meeting anyone," she said, blinking back at herself.

"No need," Nathaniel muttered, finding his voice, and deciding to get the worst over with. Despite a few errant locks having escaped their pins during her tumble inside her carriage, there was no one to notice apart from himself, and he didn't mind in the least.

Perhaps he could point that out as a distinct benefit.

"Tea and some of Cook's best biscuits, Mr. Barnes," he requested before offering Lady Patience his arm. "If you recall, the drawing room is this way."

She didn't hesitate but took hold. "Your home is as lovely as I remember."

"Thank you. Now, about my family. I believe I mentioned my sister being in *that way* and thus soon brought to bed."

"Yes," Lady Patience said. "I assumed that was why she wasn't going to Lady Kepelton's."

"Actually, Lillian is at her home in Stratford with her devoted husband by her side."

"Of course. How silly of me. Besides your mother, then, which relations have come to the seat of the earldom to celebrate the end-of-year festivities?"

"None," Nathaniel said, as they entered the sea green-and-cream room. It was large enough to have an area for sitting, another for standing, and yet a third for gaming. He brought her to one of the carved and gilded sofas situated before the tall windows, and gestured for her to sit.

Lady Patience sighed while lowering onto the gray silk with green embroidered lampas. "So only you and your mother, then?"

"Only *me*, in fact," Nathaniel said, not bothering to sit since he knew in another moment he would have to rise again.

As expected, she sprang to her feet, glancing around as if expecting others to emerge from the distant corners of the room.

"Are you saying I am alone with you?" Her countenance was one of incredulity mixed with censure.

"Hardly alone," he countered, gesturing to the bell pull that would summon an army of servants.

"You have ruined me." Her tone was a frightened whisper. "Why on earth would you bring me here, march me past your butler, who is now telling the housekeeper, who will tell the kitchen staff, who will then tell the rest that I agreed to come to your home without a companion?"

She started toward the door.

"Lady Patience, please, stop. I told Mr. Barnes, as you heard, that your carriage had tipped. And therefore, these are extraordinary circumstances. If it makes you feel any better, there are some of your own former maids and footmen working here."

Stopping in her tracks, she turned heel and cocked her head. "Are there? Why?"

"You know how servants come and go. They go from your home and they come here." Nathaniel shrugged. At that instant, his capable butler entered with a footman and maid in tow and gestured for the two to set down trays, one with a tea service and the other with far more than mere biscuits.

"Good day, milady," said the maid. "It's me, Jane Pearson."

"Yes, I can see it is you," Lady Patience replied, looking none too pleased. "And Andrew, yes?"

"Yes, milady," said the footman.

"My carriage tipped over," she explained to them.

An astonishing thing to witness as Nathaniel didn't think he had ever seen anyone of their class explain themselves to the household help before.

"Mr. Crawford was driving," Lady Patience added.

The footman nodded as if that explained everything, and the maid rolled her eyes. Nathaniel was beginning to think the man was not an experienced driver.

"That will be all," he said, and the three turned away. "A minute, Jane," he added, halting the young woman. "I would like you perform all the duties of a lady's maid for Lady Patience while she is here."

Then he looked at his guest. "If that's all right with you."

Lady Patience still appeared doubtful, but she nodded. "For the *short* period of time I am visiting due to this unforeseen emergency, that would be agreeable."

"I am pleased to do it, milady," said Jane, before curtsying and following the others out of the room.

"That doesn't change the fact that you and I are alone," Lady Patience pointed out, but her keen blue gaze had landed upon the plate of biscuits, tarts, and slices of cake. "It is unacceptable and unheard of."

"Please," he invited, "resume your seat. You can at least warm up a little. After all, the snow has been falling thickly since we arrived. No one, not the greatest prude in all of England could expect you to travel out in such weather, not even to protect your reputation."

With only the barest of hesitations, seemingly resigned to her fate, Lady Patience offered, "Shall I pour?"

"Thank you." It was all very civilized, yet decidedly strange. Nathaniel had never been in such a situation, alone with a woman who wasn't his mother or sister, in a drawing room.

Being in the private company of a female was reserved for his townhouse bedroom or one of the finer cunny warrens when he felt like venturing out and enjoying an expensive cyprian.

The lady had the right of it—a state of affairs as unheard of as milking a pigeon.

Yet despite how she'd left him confounded and, frankly, bruised to the bone a year prior, he was looking forward to the remainder of the day and especially the upcoming evening.

CHAPTER THREE

"**M**ilady, there is just one evening gown and one more day dress!"

Jane's shocked voice simply made Patience sigh. She sat on the counterpane, a blue fleece one, in a perfectly lovely bedroom with a thick blue-and-cream Persian rug underfoot. Her own chamber at St. Claire Hall used to be as fine as this, but sacrifices had been made over the past nineteen months since she'd received word of her parents' demise.

"Did you leave a trunk in the overturned carriage?" Jane persisted. "Or perhaps out in the sledge?"

"No." Patience could not explain to her maid, *Lord Beaumont's* maid, that she had planned on staying a mere one day and night at Lady Kepelton's before going home.

Desperation choked her. As lady of the house, it was her duty to feed those who still served her. And that sacred obligation weighed heavily. In the new year, last quarter's dwindling revenues from her remaining tenants-at-will and any income from holdings she hadn't been forced to sell would sustain them for another few months. It was always at the end of each quarter that they suffered.

While she didn't owe Jane an explanation, she had to say something reasonable.

"Mr. Crawford took the rest of my things back home. I brought only enough clothing until tomorrow. Lord Beaumont thought it best if we shelter here for the duration of the storm."

"Oh well, then," Jane said, satisfied. "I've put everything in the wardrobe. It's too early to change for dinner, milady. Do you need anything else?"

Directly after taking tea along with some delicious sweet treats, Patience had needed to get away from the earl. In his charming presence, it was too easy to forget that he would happily marry her for her house and land.

"I shall go downstairs again in a little while. You may leave me."

"Yes, milady." The young woman whom Patience's mother had hired as an upstairs chamber maid disappeared quickly with a soft click of the door.

Climbing onto the bed, she stretched out, appreciating the warmth in the room from the stoked fire in the hearth. At home, she had retreated into a small section of St. Claire Hall, heating merely what had to be heated to keep her and three servants from freezing.

This, however, was luxury. This was heaven. And it was by the kindness of the earl. He must want something in return. She thought back to the kiss. More than one, in truth, before she had made her way back to Lady Kepelton's well-lit drawing room a year earlier.

If her financial state didn't improve, then Patience could do worse than accept an offer from him. At least he was delightful to look at, and she knew he could arouse her passions.

However, her parents had been perfectly matched and hopelessly in love. Patience had grown up expecting the same for herself. Lord Beaumont's reputation as a rake ever since he'd left Oxford, if not before, had been bandied about in the gossip rags and on the tongues of those who attended London events.

Patience used to be one of those members of the *ton*, with her mother at her side. Sometimes both her parents had accompanied her to one of the private debutante balls during her first season. But although she had never been one to rattle on about other people's business, she'd have had to be cloth-eared not to hear whispers and outright bawdy talk about the Earl of Beaumont.

In a word, *scandalous*. He liked the ladies, and the ladies liked him. Thus, he seemed always to be escorting one or two within the same week, dancing thrice at one ball with another, and even found in a garden behind a hedge with a misguided female.

For a few days at Lady Kepelton's home, perhaps because it was her first house party since losing her parents, Patience had allowed herself to believe Lord Beaumont thought her special. Worthy of his undivided attention.

She had soon learned from Lady Priscilla Malcolm Price that what the earl truly thought was that Patience was easily persuaded.

Now, a year later, he might be correct. On the other hand, given his propensity for enjoying himself with feminine company, her life *after* marriage, while luxurious, might be a humiliating one at best.

With a groan, Patience sat up, then rose from the bed. Her hair was probably a fright, but she didn't want to ring for Jane, nor even look in the mirror. Instead, without changing, she made her way back down to the drawing room. The curtains had been closed and the lamps lit although it was not yet dusk.

The coziness made her smile. St. Claire Hall used to be liked this. Then she recalled those who awaited her. Not knowing the earl's cook, she couldn't possibly beg for food. And if she stole it out from under Lord Beaumont's own nose, Patience doubted she could transport it home.

With that miserable thought, she went to the large bowed windows at the front of the room and drew back a curtain.

"Hell's bells," she swore softly. The latest snow had piled up quickly, seemingly impassable. She was trapped.

"Beautiful to look at," came Lord Beaumont's voice.

She turned. He'd entered from the far end of the room, past a table set out for cards. His tall figure and trim physique gave her the same fluttery feeling as it had the previous year when she'd encountered him at the Twelvetide party. Indeed, as it had each time she'd seen him since he'd returned from university.

"I suppose you're right," Patience agreed. "Beautiful as long as one isn't outside in it. Then it could be deadly."

"Perhaps by morning, it will have settled enough that we can take a walk or a ride."

"On your sledge?" If the landscape was traversable, then she would go home.

"Or on horseback," he said, "if you enjoy riding."

He made it sound as though she was an invited guest at a country party. More so when he added, "Meanwhile, are you amenable to some lighthearted amusement?"

Her glance caught his, and the butterflies took flight in her stomach. What did this roguish nobleman have in mind?

"Snap Dragon would be fun," he suggested.

She couldn't help smiling at the notion of the two of them playing the group game by themselves—snatching at flaming, brandy-soaked raisins in a candlelit room. People became silly, drank as much brandy as they could, and often burned their fingers, all while chanting the accompanying song.

At her expression, Lord Beaumont added, "It is Christmas eve after all."

Standing close to him, dipping her fingers in hot brandy, and probably growing overly companionable did not seem wise at that moment.

"Maybe another time," Patience deferred. They needed to do something less casual and informal. "Would you give me a tour of your home? If memory serves me, your family owns and displays some beautiful landscapes."

"Very well," he said, "but perhaps we'll find a festive entertainment for this evening anyway."

With that loaded remark, he gestured for her to lead the way. "We shall start in the east gallery." And they began to climb the stairs.

"*Here he comes with flaming bowl, Don't he mean to take his toll, Snip! Snap! Dragon!*"

"What is that you're singing?" he asked.

"Nothing," she said quickly. But she had been quietly chanting the catchy tune.

"You were!" Lord Beaumont insisted, sounding delighted. "You were thinking of Snap Dragon, and now it is stuck in your head. *Take care you don't take too much, Be not greedy in your clutch, Snip! Snap! Dragon!*"

When he finished the stanza, Patience switched to humming the familiar song, having grown too shy to sing the words.

The earl didn't seem to have the same problem and continued, "*With his blue and lapping tongue, Many of you will be stung, Snip! Snap! Dragon!* I won't say that line ever again without thinking of your blue eyes, as vivid as any brandy flame."

Lapping tongue, indeed! Her cheeks felt warm as if they were playing the game instead of cresting the top of the staircase and strolling toward one of Lord Beaumont's art collections.

Abruptly, he took her arm and threaded it under his. While that was entirely appropriate for a public promenade, there, in a long, private gallery, it caused shivers of tingling awareness to dance down her spine. Patience could smell his spicy cologne. The alluring fragrance brought her back to their first kiss as if it had only just occurred.

All she had to do was stop walking and turn toward him. He would take her in his arms. Instead, she wrenched free, hurrying forward and away from him.

"Lady Prudence, what is your hurry?" he asked, his voice echoing slightly in the otherwise empty hallway.

"Lady *Patience*," she corrected over her shoulder through gritted teeth. He thought her prudent, too much so, because she wouldn't play a somewhat risky game, nor walk arm-in-arm while the sides of their bodies brushed with every step.

"Dreadful name," he said, a smile in his voice.

Lord Beaumont was correct, and she couldn't gainsay him, so she said nothing. But she entirely agreed that *patience* was a terrible thing to force on a person by way of a name. As a child, it had made her more impatient than any normal person, simply so she didn't have to live up to the label.

Yet she'd grown up a great deal in the past nineteen months since her parents' passing. And she liked to think she was, in fact, more patient.

"Middle name?" the earl prompted when she slowed her steps and began to admire the paintings hanging on either side of her.

No one ever asked her since no one used it. Lord Beaumont caught up, and she couldn't help glancing at him. At her hesitation, he raised a dark eyebrow.

"Don't tell me it is something equally awful like Honora or Modesty. Although Grace would suit you," he mused with a tilt of his head that made her want to sink her fingers into his hair, raise herself upon tiptoe, and kiss him soundly.

"No, it's none of those. And please do not make fun because I quite like it," she said, and then told him what it was. "Russell."

"Excuse me?" he shot back.

"Russell," she repeated, lifting her chin.

"To do with your red hair?" He asked. "Like *rusty* or *russet?*"

"Of course not! My mother's maiden name, 'tis all."

"*Hmm*. Patience Russell St. Claire. Then *Russ* you shall be."

"I shall not," she said, gaping.

"You cannot stop me." His merry expression challenged her to try.

Making a face, she grabbed her skirts in both hands and lifted every layer so she could stride quickly away from him. *The nerve of the man, calling her Russ!*

"You may not go around renaming people to suit you," she said over her shoulder.

"But Russ is sweet and short, and far better than Patience. I suppose Chance would be another option."

She kept walking until she was at the other end of the hallway. Taking a quick left turn, Patience found another long corridor stretched before her. All the while, he followed. Eventually, she slowed down again before stopping to examine a large winter landscape with opposing battalions trudging knee-deep in snow toward each other. The earl came to stand beside her.

"It looks like us earlier when I rescued you."

She glanced at him, then back at the painting. "Really? How so?"

"We have an adversarial relationship, do we not?" he asked.

His lordship was correct, and suddenly, after holding onto a generous dose of outrage toward him for a year, it seemed unnecessary.

"Let us stop," she said. "Being adversaries, I mean. At least until after I leave." A short truce until the morrow would be easy.

His gaze swept her face and settled upon her mouth.

"Yes, let's," he agreed. "Do you know *my* given name?"

Why were her cheeks heating at the thought? "I do."

"Say it," he commanded, surprising her.

Clearing her throat, she muttered, "Nathaniel. And what kind of name is that?" *A stupid remark,* Patience thought, but she was still smarting over how he had dismissed her own.

"A very good, solid, ordinary name, I believe. But you may call me Nate, if you wish."

"Highly improper. I must call you Lord Beaumont."

He shrugged. "Must you?"

"Or by your family name." She smiled slightly at the notion of constantly calling him Lord Murray-Savile, as he was known before he obtained the earldom.

"Russ," he said softly.

She swallowed, her mouth unexpectedly dry due to his husky tone. She fell captive to his leaf-green eyes and waited for what was to come.

"Your smile is beautiful, even such a small one, and despite how it appeared for reasons of which I know not."

Patience had nothing to say as the air around them sizzled, nor could she move an inch if someone cracked a whip beside her. His attractive lips formed the words, "You may continue to 'my lord' me. But I prefer Nate."

She preferred Nate, too. Rather, she preferred *him!*

Then he kissed her. As easy as falling off a bridge, their mouths were fused. Patience tasted the lemon cake they'd eaten, and his luxurious fragrance intoxicated her more than any wine.

With her insides humming and fluttering like a beehive, she opened her mouth to his questing tongue. His stroked hers, and she returned the favor. In a heartbeat, his hands were upon her waist, pulling her closer, and Patience was helpless to resist. So much for her reputation!

When he tilted his head, slanting his mouth across hers, she simply had to touch him. Sliding her hands up the front of him until she could lace her fingers behind his neck, finally, she touched his silky, thick hair. *Like a pelt,* she mused.

Her body tingled, and she couldn't contain the soft moan that escaped her.

Ladies did not do this. That thought flitted through her brain and swiftly disappeared. Relaxing against him, she relished the heat and strength of his body cradling her curves.

At her surrender, Lord Beaumont groaned and pressed her back against the painting.

"*Ow,*" she said as the opulent frame dug into her spine.

At once, the kiss ended as quickly as it had begun.

CHAPTER FOUR

I mmediately, Nathaniel stepped back, bringing her with him.

"Blasted gallery," he exclaimed looking right and left. There was very little free wall space upon which he could press a willing female.

"It is no matter." Slipping from his grasp, Lady Patience started walking again. "I believe I shall go to my room and have a rest before dinner."

The devil! She had come to her senses, and he had been correct—they were prudent senses, to be sure.

"We have barely begun the tour," he reminded her. "What's more, we just ate, and dinner is hours away."

"Nonetheless," Patience said, firmly. "It is for the best."

"What if I vow to keep my hands *and* my mouth off of you?"

The sound of nervous laughter bubbled up from her soft, sweet lips. It was true that speaking aloud of such things was outrageous. Maybe frightening for her.

"Please, Russ," he beseeched. "I will behave."

"You misbehave this very instant by addressing me thusly."

He tried to look remorseful and undoubtedly failed. What was more, he didn't feel an ounce of regret over the kiss. Be that as it may, he must get them back on a civilized footing.

"Let us continue the tour," he offered again.

She hesitated, then said, "As long as there shall be no more touching, not even linking of arms."

Purposefully, to lighten the mood, he heaved a sigh that was almost comical in length before gesturing for her to continue.

"Very well. Let us proceed, but at a slower pace. You missed many fine pieces worthy of your inspection in the last gallery."

With temptation dogging their steps, they continued in one another's company for an hour more. Then another. Not only viewing his family's art collection, he also gave her a tour of the manor's layout. By its conclusion, she had become lost more than once.

"There are so many rooms," she said, "I scarcely have time to do more than poke my head into most, each one well-furnished and beautiful."

"I should charge admittance and offer tours daily," he quipped. "That would fatten the coffers, having people coming to gape at Beaumont Manor."

"*You* are quite gape-worthy," Lady Patience said, making him laugh until he realized it was the nicest compliment she'd yet given him.

"You are far more gape-worthy, Russ. Your flame hair alone is worth the price of admission."

Her delightful freckled cheeks pinkened. It struck him that she ought to have been scooped up during the season, but she hadn't been in London. Nor the prior one because her parents had passed away.

"Did you ever have a season?" he asked.

"Of course." That lovely chin lifted with pride. "I had two."

"I'm sorry I was not at any of the same events. I've spent time on the Continent, back and forth over the past few years, often during London's high season."

"I do not believe you were away when I was last in London," Lady Patience said carefully, giving him the idea that she knew more about his whereabouts than he had known of hers. "In fact, I did see you at one or two private balls."

Nathaniel was flabbergasted. "Why didn't you make yourself known to me? After all, we are neighbors."

Her glance fell to the floor, then rose. "Naturally, my parents kept me with the other debutantes, and you were not one of the gentlemen who asked me to dance."

She was correct that he rarely waded into the pool of young chits, all eager for an engagement their first year in public. They were like unfinished sculptures, where he preferred those more polished and worldly. Moreover, he hadn't been out to ruin anyone, and thus, when he attended balls, he stayed in the shark-infested waters of the experienced ladies, some married, some widowed.

In the years in which he had not been in a marrying state of mind, Nathaniel had a penchant for a certain type of female who wasn't as constricted by society's rules, nor necessarily as eager for a husband.

Everything had changed for him with his father's passing. And a year ago, in a dunderheaded fashion, he had believed he could use the same seductive tactics on this particular young lady. He ought to have shown restraint and courted her properly.

The devil take him if he hadn't gone about it all wrong again. Why, he'd just backed her up against a painting! Vowing to himself he would do better, even if his baser side was thrumming and throbbing for her, Nathaniel admired his own noble resolve.

"Would you care to return to your room now? Maybe a hot bath to soothe any aches from your earlier mishap, and then I shall let you alone until dinner."

Her blue eyes widened. "Yes," she said. "I would love a hot bath. A deep one, if possible."

The lady said it as though it were a nicety she couldn't have any time she wished. How odd!

"Not at all. How selfish of me! I wasn't the one turned topsy-turvy in a carriage. Speaking of which, yours is already in my carriage house being mended."

He witnessed the relief flooding her features.

"You look as though I just told you I had rescued your baby."

"I am greatly relieved," she said, "mostly for the carriage mending but also for the bath. I don't suppose you have any floral-scented salts or oils."

An image of her bare form, wet and glistening with oil as she rose from a tub of steaming water made him instantly hard. Turning heel so she wouldn't see his arousal, he cleared his throat.

"This way. I'll lead you back to your bedroom door and send for Jane. I'm sure she'll know all about salts and oils and the like."

It was his turn to hurry along the hallway, as she strode to keep up.

In a few minutes, Lady Patience was safely behind her bedroom door, and after instructing his staff to boil water and sending the maid to the lady's chamber, he went to his study.

As he sat before the fire, he mused upon what he wanted. *To bed her?* Most definitely. But more. He wanted to woo her properly. He hoped to discover why she'd rumped him last year and then spurned his advances. What better way to accomplish both than to keep her under his roof for the Twelvetide?

Outrageous perhaps, but a gamble that, if it paid off, would reap him a lifetime of returns.

First, however, something was niggling at his brain. Rising, he pulled the cord and took his seat again. In a very short time, his butler appeared.

"Who was the last of our staff to come from the St. Claire estate? Send him or her to me at once."

PATIENCE SOAKED IN THE tub so long the ends of her fingers had become like prunes. Halfway through, Jane had needed to use a bucket to bail out some of the tepid water and make room for newly boiled. It was heaven, as were the bath salts.

Her skin was soft and fragrant, and she was truly warm right down to her bones for the first time since the weather had become frigid weeks earlier.

Yet her mind was tormented. The earl mentioned fat coffers reminding Patience that her staff was growing leaner both in number and in health, and that her own coffers were as thin as parchment.

But his kiss had been exquisite, better even than she had recalled. Sinfully, it left her wanting more. More kisses, more touching, much more of him. She'd been right to end it and not let him hold her arm again.

What would seem normal next? Allowing him to bed her?

"Time to dress, milady," Jane said, probably so Patience didn't ask for more hot water.

Since there was only one choice of gown for evening, it was not difficult to decide what to wear. Thick, cotton-lined, blue satin with silver piping and trim, the dress had puffy, *en gigot* sleeves, down to her wrists. And although her upper chest was exposed, she knew Beaumont Manor would be warm enough that she had no need of a shawl.

Jane brushed out Patience's hair, braided it, and put it up in a coiled bun with gentle ringlets on either side. Without a familiar enough relationship with the maid to consult her, Patience looked in the long mirror.

Will I do? she silently asked her reflection.

The gown was two seasons old, but Patience had no worries the earl would know about such things. The largest change might be that her sleeves were a little puffier than the current fashion. Thus, she nodded.

"May I show you the way, milady?"

"I know how to reach the drawing room."

"His lordship thought that room too drafty for this evening, milady. He will meet you in the lavender salon."

Patience thought of the long and overwhelming tour. "Then I guess you had best lead me, Jane."

The room was empty when Patience arrived. It was a small, interior chamber with no exterior windows. A fire blazed merrily in the tiled hearth, a wall sconce was lit on either side of the room's two entryways, and lamps were dotted around the room. Cheerful, warm. Intimate. She swallowed.

"How thoughtful of the earl," she said, but Jane had vanished. Taking a seat on the damask sofa, Patience folded her hands in her lap and put her head back to wait.

When she opened her eyes, Lord Beaumont was seated beside her drinking red wine.

"Oh!" she startled, dabbing at her mouth with her fingertips in case she'd drooled. Luckily, her chin was dry.

"My apologies, my lord. Why didn't you awaken me?"

"When a lady looks so beautiful in slumber," he said, "it would be a crime to disturb her. Even your soft snoring was melodic."

Just like that, he had her laughing again. The charming earl with the roguish reputation was being more humorous than seductive. *Thank goodness!* One could hardly leap from a compliment about snoring to kissing passionately.

So why had her thoughts made the leap?

"Would you care for a glass of wine?" he offered. "Mulled or plain?"

Since a carafe of wine was before them on the low table, she didn't wish for the fuss of sending to the kitchen for heated, spiced wine.

"This will do nicely," she said, and he poured her a glass, setting it on the table rather than handing it to her. Their fingers did not so much as brush.

"How was your bath?" he asked, then immediately shook his head. "My apologies for such an impertinent question. The state of your bath is your own business, nor do I wish to imply that I was pondering you taking one."

Oh dear. His lordship seemed perturbed. Patience could only imagine he had decided to be as proper as possible . . . and was failing.

She smiled to put him at ease. They spent a very pleasant half hour discussing their mutual acquaintances in the area. At dinner, eaten in the formal dining room with both of them at one end of the table, they talked about the village. By dessert, they were discussing the local farmers and the state of their county's road system and agricultural prosperity.

Upon returning to the salon after dinner, Patience was full of nourishment and knowledge. And guilt. While she was enjoying Beaumont luxury, her maid, cook, and footman were cold and hungry.

"I promise I won't suggest Snap Dragon again," the earl said, interrupting her dark thoughts, "but perhaps a friendly game of cards or chess. And I would like a glass of mulled wine now. Would you?"

Thus, they stayed up until eleven, when Patience could no longer hide her yawning, nor keep her heavy eyelids completely open.

Lord Beaumont accompanied her to the foot of the staircase, still not touching her, but when she turned to bid him good night, apparently he couldn't help himself. Taking her hand, he bowed over it.

"Happy Christmas eve to you, my lady."

"And to you, my lord. I thank you for rescuing me and for offering such grand hospitality."

"Without you, I would have spent my day and evening alone so you have more than repaid me." He released her hand. "Sleep well, . . . Russ."

She clucked her tongue and waggled a finger. "A pity, Lord Beaumont. You were behaving so well, too."

With his laughter in her ears, she left him. Halfway up the stairs, Patience turned to see that he was still watching her. A shiver of awareness ran down her spine, yet she kept climbing. It was easy to picture the green-eyed devil coming to her bedroom in the middle of the night, tapping at the door, and slipping into the room.

Then into her bed. Country parties were notorious for such mischief, or so she'd heard.

If he were such a bold rake, she would have to find the strength to resist. To do elsewise was unthinkable.

Sighing, Patience found her way to her room and once inside, leaned against the door. Men and women did not spend the night under the same roof *without* a chaperone. And now, she knew why. Every inclination of her being was to kiss him . . . and more.

A part of her hoped he would play the libertine and come to her. After all, no one would believe that Lord Beaumont and, by association, Lady Patience were comporting themselves respectably.

They were gaining nothing by exercising restraint, except frustration. And with each passing year of her life, her curiosity grew to experience *the act.*

On the other hand, she would maintain her self-respect, which would have to keep her company. Thank goodness tomorrow she would be away from the temptation of Nathaniel Beaumont.

Patience nearly jumped out of her skin at a tap upon her door.

"Yes?"

"Milady, may I help you undress and take down your hair?"

Patience chuckled at her wild imaginings, then bid Jane enter to help her get swiftly into bed.

CHAPTER FIVE

Patience had slept soundly with her full stomach and in a warm bed. Even the now cold hearth and rapidly cooling room didn't wake her from her slumber. Not until the sun came through the smallest opening between her bed hangings, slanting across her face, did she rouse.

Yawning, for a moment, she forgot where she was. Then came the guilt, followed by the familiar gutting fear. How could she keep her home? If her luck didn't change, she would lose everything.

"Merry Christmas, milady." Jane sounded cheerful when she answered the bell-pull, despite it being simply another day of work.

If Jane could be happy, then Patience, who had so much more—well, currently not that much more of anything except debt and prospects—then who was she not to be happy? And grateful.

"Merry Christmas, Jane."

"Are you ready to dress and eat your breakfast?"

"Indeed, I am." Despite having more to eat the day before than she had in a long while, her stomach was already grumbling and ready for more.

"We've all eaten a special Christmas meal below stairs, milady. Now it's yours and his lordship's turn."

But Patience was distracted by noises outside her window. "What's going on outside?"

"Lord Beaumont hadn't intended to decorate, what with going to Lady Kepelton's party and since the Dowager Countess Beaumont isn't here, either. However, now that you're staying for the Twelvetide, his lordship asked us to begin decorating. Some of the footmen are outside gathering holly boughs and mistletoe and bringing in one of Queen Charlotte's beloved evergreen trees—may she rest in peace. Such a nice tradition, isn't it, milady?"

Patience had stopped listening. *What did Jane mean?* When the maid took a breath, Patience got a word in edgeways.

"I am leaving after breakfast, Jane. I'm going home."

"Oh well, milady. That's not what I heard."

"What you heard?" Patience frowned. "From whom?"

The maid must have realized she was gossiping and spouting hearsay, so she closed her mouth tightly and shrugged.

"Hurry, Jane, my gown," Patience commanded.

Very soon afterward, she had sailed out of the room ahead of the maid, although Jane quickly caught up to her in the main entrance hall where the manor staff was running hither and yon with greenery and thick ribbons.

"What a hullabaloo," Patience muttered, but it gave her a happy feeling inside.

"This way, milady." Jane steered her in the direction of a sunny salon. On the threshold, Patience paused at the sight of a table already laden with every imaginable breakfast item.

She nearly swooned. There was enough to feed ten, never mind two.

Lord Beaumont was already seated before the feast, drinking chocolate if her nose detected correctly. He rose to his feet.

"You had a good, long sleep," he said. "I hope you don't mind some of the hot food is now lukewarm."

"That matters not," she assured him, taking a seat. "Please, sit and eat. I apologize for keeping you waiting."

"No apology is necessary, Russ. I called for breakfast too soon. I hope Jane didn't wake you."

"Please don't call me Russ," she said. "The sun awakened me, as I was abed longer than I had a right to be. I intend to eat some of this food, tepid or not, and then I must return to my home."

"Impossible. By the way, merry Christmas."

Patience was helping herself from the platters of coddled eggs, sausages, thick bacon, and stewed tomatoes. She took a piece of cold, hard toast, too, a small fried oatcake, and some thinly sliced sauteed potatoes.

"Merry Christmas," she returned. Then she ate half of what was on her plate and drank a cup of chocolate in silence so as not to speak with her mouth full. She refused to gainsay him, but she intended to leave.

Finally, she spooned into a bowl some fruit preserved in thick syrup that must have been prepared and saved in the growing season. It was divine!

When she refilled her cup from the chocolate pot, she realized Lord Beaumont was staring at her. Quickly, she snatched her linen napkin from her lap and dabbed at her mouth.

"Better?" she asked, thinking she must have had food on her face.

"I am not sure I've ever seen a female eat such a hearty breakfast," he said. "Bravo! You shall have all the fortitude for a long day of fun."

"I have all the fortitude to ride home upon your excellent sledge," she said.

"Impossible," he repeated. "This afternoon, the villagers are coming to see the decorations and the evergreen that is this very minute standing stately in the great room."

"What has that to do with me?" Patience asked.

"Everything, Russ. I would never have sent word to the village if you hadn't inspired me. The tree will have candles, fruit, sweetmeats and, if we can manage it, some pennies tied in handkerchiefs and other knickknacks, although it is too late to make or purchase any toys."

He sounded sincerely sad about that. "Still, we can give them a good Christmas for a few hours and send them all home at least with some of Cook's biscuits and buns."

"I must go home at once," Patience said. "I cannot be seen here."

"I sent the invitation jointly from both our estates. You are my hostess for the day."

She frowned. "You ought to have asked me." Would Mr. Crawford hear of it and at least come on foot for some food? She hoped so.

"How will people come here? I thought you said the snow was too deep."

"The sun is out. Snow is melting a little, and our villagers are not weaklings. They're used to getting around on horseback, sledge, or by foot. We shall ask those who come if they know of anyone sick or infirm, and send a sledge out with some food."

"Then tonight, I shall take that same sledge and return home," she insisted.

"On Christmas?" Lord Beaumont looked shocked. "You would leave me alone on Christmas and not share a festive dinner with me? How cruel! After all I've done for you, too."

When he put it that way, she sounded ungrateful.

"Very well. I shall stay another night."

The earl smiled smugly and drained his second cup of chocolate. Meanwhile, you may oversee the decorations, or help as you wish." All at once, he snapped his fingers.

"We have to find a yule log. Something already dead, or it won't catch fire."

"You're too late," she reminded him. Everyone knew that one brought in a log on Christmas eve.

He waved away her protest. "We shall light it with the villagers. It will be a grand addition to the party."

Patience liked his boyish eagerness. "Did you save a piece from last year's log with which to light it?"

His expression lost a little gaiety. "I don't know." Then he brightened. "Mr. Barnes will know. If we don't, we shall grab an old stick and pretend."

"I suppose that will suffice," she agreed. "Shall we go see how the decorations are proceeding? I like a little of everything: ivy, holly, laurel, box, yew, and mistletoe."

"Then let us make sure we have a little of everything," the earl agreed. "But first, the yule log."

He rose to his feet, and she joined him, understanding why he wore a festive red cravat and a red-and-gold waistcoat under his coat.

"Is what I'm wearing suitable for performing duties as hostess?" She thought of all the gowns she could have brought from home.

Lord Beaumont gave her a long look, head to toe. Patience nearly gasped at the tingling throughout her body. Not only that, her skin grew tighter, especially over her breasts—a most disconcerting sensation.

"You look perfect," he said, and the tingling became a sizzle. *Good gracious, what this man's green gaze could do to her!*

They spent the remainder of the morning making everything as festive as possible. When the villagers arrived by early afternoon, the earl himself poured wine over the yule log, but gave the honor of lighting it to the eldest living member of the community.

A wizened old man, whom Patience recognized as a farmer her father used to vow made the best cider, hobbled forward, leaning on a shoulder-high stick. He was flanked by young men who looked to be his grandsons.

"That's a fine-looking yule log, milord," the farmer said loudly. Without further preamble, neither bombastic speech nor prayer for the upcoming year, the old man touched the flaming twig to the log, and it erupted at one end in merry flames.

Everyone cheered, and the grandsons escorted him back to a chair before beginning to ladle cups of cider from a cask for any who wished. Patience sent up a silent *merry Christmas* to her parents and enjoyed a cup of the sharp, tangy brew.

"IT WAS A SUCCESSFUL Christmas," Nathaniel said, stretching out his legs and crossing his ankles. It was, perhaps, rather too-relaxed a posture, but Russ, as he now thought of her, was also leaning back on her end of the sofa with her eyes closed.

They had hosted fifty villagers at least. And everyone had been happy despite not having any toys for the little ones. It turned out children were just as happy with oranges and figs, with biscuits and honeyed nuts, and certainly, with copper coins.

And the adults enjoyed a large quantity of mulled wine, cider, fruitcake, and the chance to sit in the Beaumont Manor great room, an impressive chamber with a vaulted ceiling and a stained-glass clerestory running the length of the roof line on either side.

"Very successful," the flame-haired lady beside him agreed without opening her eyelids.

Nathaniel wanted to move closer, but he was determined to court her slowly. One kiss a day if she would let him. Maybe a little more if he could get away with it.

People had stayed longer than he'd predicted. And now, it was past the usual dinnertime, and they still wore their day clothes, and neither felt like moving, let alone changing and going into the dining room.

"You were an excellent hostess," he told her. "Everywhere at once, while effortlessly making everyone welcome. I noticed how much everyone enjoyed your company."

Still, she didn't open her eyes. "Thank you. And you, as well, my lord."

"Me as well, what, my lady?"

"I don't know. I think I consumed too much wine today since everyone wished to toast to Father Christmas."

"Are you hungry? I know you usually are famished."

She hesitated, then opened her eyes. Their stunning blue stole his breath.

"I could eat a morsel of two." Then what he could only think of as a dark shadow crossed over her features. "I had hoped to see some of my own staff. Did you send an invitation to the Hall?"

"I'm sorry, I did not." He ought to tell her that he had sent a better parcel to St. Claire Hall, but he wasn't sure she would appreciate what he had done. She might feel as though he had overstepped.

Rising slowly, Nathaniel tugged the bell-pull twice and then sat down again. Soon, they were eating hot food from trays while remaining seated in the salon.

"This is a unique experience," Lady Patience said.

They each had but a single large dinner plate with a helping of roast duck, roasted carrots, boiled potatoes with cream, and his cook's marvelously delicious seasoned stuffing. Nearly everything on their plates was smothered in gravy.

"Indeed," he agreed, glad he was having the experience with her. The fire crackled, and he couldn't think of anywhere he would rather be.

"Yet this isn't a proper Christmas dinner," he pointed out. "My staff expected us in the dining room and were prepared to bring out platter after platter."

"Is your cook angry?" Russ asked, before popping another bite into her lovely mouth.

"Probably. But maybe not. One can never tell." He thought it highly likely Cook had already tippled her fair share of wine and was ready to enjoy Boxing Day with her feet up. "Do you think you will still be awake for supper?"

"I do not believe so, if you don't mind too much."

"Not at all." Nathaniel set his tray on the table in front of him, having cleared his plate. "I suppose you are too tired for Snap Dragon."

Lady Patience laughed, a delightful sound. "In my present state, I will be burned for sure."

Then she fell silent a moment before adding, "On the other hand, I would like to play since I have nothing else to give you for Christmas, and you have provided me with food and shelter, as well as a splendid party."

Something inside him shifted, like a burning log falling in a fireplace. He was starting to think this woman was everything he had ever wanted. She had already given him a great gift for Christmas, the pleasure of her company. However, he wouldn't pass up her continued presence and a game involving brandy.

Jumping up, he tugged the bell-pull again. This time, he ordered preparations in the lavender salon for the silly game.

"Ten minutes, Mr. Barnes, and we shall be in there to test our mettle."

"Yes, my lord." His butler had been utterly unruffled by the day's deluge of people, and he seemed equally ready to indulge his employer in whatever Christmas amusement he desired.

A few more hours, and the entire staff would have the rest of the night off as well as all the following day. The house would have to run itself.

When Russ had finished eating, Nathaniel lifted the tray from her lap, careful not to touch her thighs, and placed it beside his own. Then he offered her his hand.

"Are you good at playing Snap Dragon?" he asked.

"I am passing fair. And yourself?"

He was too competitive, even at a meaningless game, but he would try to tame his ruthless nature and let her win.

CHAPTER SIX

"**I** cannot believe I have won yet again," Russ said, holding out her palm with the plump, hot raisin steaming upon it. Nathaniel hadn't eaten a single one yet, while she had managed to grab three! Moreover, he hadn't *let* her win, not once.

"Are your fingers made of steel, my lady?"

She laughed, and despite the dim light, purposefully lit only around the room's edges for the sake of the game, he could see her eyes flashing blue as the flaming brandy in the bowl between them.

Lady Patience looked like one of Hamlet's witches—except exceedingly beautiful. In good humor, she began to sing:

> *"For he snaps at all that comes,*
> *Snatching at his feast of plums,*
> *Snip! Snap! Dragon!"*

"Ready?" she asked. Without waiting for his answer, she reached toward the bowl and snatched another raisin from the hot liquor.

"*Ouch,*" she said, but she had it. This time, she grabbed for Nathaniel's hand and place the treat upon his palm before singing the next verse:

"But Old Christmas makes him come,
Though he looks so fee! fa! fum!
Snip! Snap! Dragon!"

"Try again," she urged. "What are *your* fingers made of? Custard?" Russ laughed at her own joke. She was well and truly tipsy.

Nathaniel shook his head, not minding losing to her one bit. He would let her win his last farthing at cards or hobble his horse if he raced against her, whatever it took to keep such a happy look beaming up at him.

Still, he had to make an effort and redeem himself, if merely to save face. Peering into the copper tureen, he sang softly:

"Don't 'ee fear him but be bold.
Out he goes his flames are cold,
Snip! Snap! Dragon!"

And then he nodded to her. They reached out at the same time, and he felt a raisin in his grasp. He also felt her fingers, but when they lifted their hands, neither had claimed the prize.

"Ah well, my lord," she said. "At least, as the song says, his flames are growing colder." Picking up the ladle provided by his thoughtful staff, she filled a mug for each of them, complete with raisins floating atop his best brandy.

"I'm glad we played," she said. "It made this Christmas as fine as five pence."

"It properly capped the day," he agreed.

They took seats in the room lit only by four candles around its perimeter and remained in companionable silence until she said, "Tomorrow, I shall leave directly after breakfast."

His heart sank. He pondered his arguments. "On Boxing Day? With all the staff left to their own devices, it will be a difficult time to get the sledge prepared. The horses won't be ready for anything but their own day off."

She gave him a look over the edge of her cup, an auburn eyebrow raised. "Nonetheless, I must go home tomorrow."

"We shall see," he said, fighting the urge to move closer and kiss her, to taste the brandy upon her lips.

Then he thought, *why fight it?* He would enjoy another Christmas gift. To that end, he scooted closer along the sofa.

"What are you doing, Lord Beaumont?" But her tone was thick as honey and more welcoming than not.

"I am sitting companionably near the loveliest lady I know."

She sighed. "The brandy is talking as much as you. We have guzzled and whipped off our share."

"Such talk from you," he said, wondering at her knowledge of slang, while setting down his cup on the table in front of the sofa. In truth, there was a mere mouthful left at the bottom. "Even if I were sober as an executioner, I would say the same."

Reaching up, he snagged one of her curled locks between his fingers. "Soft as silk."

To his surprise, she raised her hand and her fingers took hold of the ends of his hair. "Soft as fox fur," she said.

Hm, he liked this game. "Eyes like a cloudless July sky."

She arched a single eyebrow again and tilted her head while considering her next words. The small movement was one of the most enticing he'd ever seen, and it sent a rush of heat through his body.

"Eyes like polished emeralds," Russ countered.

Nathaniel could do better. "Lips of luscious cherry satin."

She blinked, then frowned. "Cherry *satin*?"

He shrugged. "A perfect description, I would say."

Russ sipped the last of her brandy and set her cup down next to his. "*Um* . . . lopsided lips of stubborn, proud, mischievous velvet."

He couldn't help the laughter that burst from him. Then he went over the words in his head. "Lopsided?"

Suddenly, her fingers were touching his face. "Yes. This side goes only to here when you smile, but this side goes as far as here."

She must be utterly groggified to touch him so boldly. He caught her hand and brought it to his mouth, lopsided lips and all. Placing a kiss in the center of her palm, all the while, he kept his gaze on hers.

Her lashes fluttered, and her lips parted slightly, the latest most alluring thing he'd ever had the pleasure to witness. Releasing her hand, he lowered his head and claimed her cherry satin, sucking her lower lip between his.

Careful not to overwhelm, he didn't press her back or try to maneuver her into lying down. He didn't touch her at all with his hands, solely with his mouth. The kiss went on and on, he tilted his head to one side, and when he had his fill, he slanted the other way.

Russ met him at each juncture, stroking his tongue with hers until he was hard as a flagpole. He didn't mind the discomfort behind the fall front of his trousers. He would kiss this woman all night if he could. *Tortured groin be damned!*

Eventually, however, she made a mewing sound that wrapped around his heart and squeezed it while his arousal throbbed. Her hands went to his coat, either to pull him closer or to stave off his advances. He didn't know, as they merely rested there.

In either case, Nathaniel backed away and rose to his feet, despite his entire body aching, coiled with need and frustration.

"Let me escort you to the staircase," he offered, drawing her to her feet. He didn't dare take her any farther, certainly not to her bedroom door.

Her petal-soft lips were indeed like cherries now, very red and a little puffy. She said nothing. He had no doubt she was as stunned and stimulated as he was.

Moreover, Russ treated him to a particularly exaggerated sway of her hips while she climbed the main staircase. *The minx!*

Enjoying her sauciness, he watched her ascend while catching a goodly glimpse of her ankles. Sometimes being rumped was a pleasure.

When she turned the corner, after sending him a last lingering glance, he stretched broadly, reaching his arms toward the high foyer ceiling with its impressive plaster design. Then he yawned, nearly splitting his face. He, too, was tired. Nevertheless, before he turned in for the night, he would confirm with his butler that his earlier plan had come to fruition.

For he was certain when the deceased Lord and Lady St. Claire had been alive, their estate was profitable and its inhabitants wanted for nothing. Certainly, no one was hungry or cold, as he'd learned from Oliver, the last man to come knocking at Nathaniel's servants' entrance after leaving his neighbor's employ.

Due to the groom's forthright disclosure, Nathaniel had known to send food that morning to St. Claire Hall. And since he had a footman who dearly wished to spend Boxing Day in London, he'd also been able to send a letter to his lawyer, carried by the eager servant on Christmas afternoon.

Nathaniel had questions that needed to be asked and answered, such as why St. Claire Hall was in such a wretched state.

CHAPTER SEVEN

A fter Patience pulled the bell for the second time and waited another seven minutes, she realized it was Boxing Day. Like any good employer, Lord Beaumont had undoubtedly presented each one of his staff with a package of whatever the butler and housekeeper had deemed most desirable, and given them all the day off.

To be even a sliver as good of an employer, Patience had to stuff her bags with food—and maybe a few candles and a jug of wine—and go home. Putting on the dress she'd arrived in, she met the earl downstairs in the breakfast salon.

He set down his cup of chocolate and rose at once. "Mr. Barnes kindly put out chocolate and toast before telling me we were on our own. Can you cook?"

Distracted by seeing Nathaniel Beaumont again after what had occurred the night before—at least a quarter hour of kissing, which Patience vowed felt like they were sharing hearts and souls—she faltered.

"A little. Enough so I wouldn't starve." Speaking of which, she urged herself to get on with it. Given the day, it was the most fortuitous time to purloin from the manor's kitchen.

Or she could simply ask him for assistance, but then Lord Beaumont would know her dire circumstances. The upper hand along with all the power would be his.

"You are wearing the same gown," he said. "The one you arrived in." A moment later, he shook his head, and she vowed his cheeks reddened. "My sincere apologies, my lady. I have grown too familiar in manner and speech. It is only that I noted your clothing two days ago because you looked so becoming in deep blue, and do so again. And I make mention of it now because at house parties, ladies never wear the same thing twice."

"Yes, I am aware of that," Patience agreed, not offended by his familiarity. His lordship liked her in blue. *Interesting.* "I told you I hadn't planned on staying the entire time at Lady Kepelton's, either."

"Why was that? I believe I asked you before." His green gaze, shimmering with curiosity, held hers.

Tongue-tied and empty-headed of excuses, she could think of no reason but the truth, which she would not tell him. Nor was she obliged to. "I prefer not to say. My business is precisely that. My own."

Pouring herself a cup of chocolate under his intense scrutiny, Patience added, "I told you last night that I must depart today."

"Not to be a croaker," his lordship said, "but I told you that Boxing Day was a poor day to do anything."

She sighed and decided to leave with or without his consent.

"Very well." She took a piece of toast, buttered it, and spread gooseberry jam thickly across it. Then she took another. After all, once back at St. Claire Hall, this would be a tantalizing memory, and she would regret not having filled her belly.

Maybe she could find a jar of jam to take home, too.

When they had finished their quiet breakfast, Lord Beaumont seemed intent on keeping her company.

"The skies are heavy with what's coming later, but meanwhile, since the sun is out, don your heavy cloak and hat, and we'll take a stroll around the property. I have an orangery, you know."

"I learned of it when I was here before, but I haven't seen it." It wouldn't matter whether she left directly or an hour hence, so Patience agreed to accompany him.

Soon, they were trudging around the property, using the paths shoveled out by grooms and footmen.

"Beaumont Manor seems even bigger when walking around its exterior," Patience remarked.

That made her host laugh. In a quarter of an hour, they had rounded the front and the side and reached the orangery. About a hundred yards from the back terrace of the main house, the building was built of stone piers and cast iron, with a Coade stone balustrade along the roofline.

And glass—pane upon pane of it.

Up three stone steps, along a gravel path, up six more steps, they stood before the orangery.

"I can count thirty panes of glass in each frame," Patience said, looking at the marvel.

"And thirty-two frames," Lord Beaumont added, "along each of the long sides. That is a great amount of expensive glass. Not a place to throw stones."

She smiled at that.

They entered the deserted and quiet building through a door at one end. Inside, Patience wanted to giggle with the joy of being warm in December.

"How is it heated?" she asked, unfastening her cloak and pulling off her fur-lined gloves.

"Pipes run under the stone blocks at our feet," Lord Beaumont said. "They have holes in them. The pipes, I mean, not our feet. I have a gardener whose job it is to stoke the brazier, sending steam through those pipes."

"Ingenious," she said.

He shrugged. "I didn't invent it. My family is merely lucky enough to have the money to build the orangery and enjoy its fruits."

Walking the length of it, the earl pointed out the many treasures.

"Naturally, we grow Spanish orange trees. We also have figs and grapes, apricots, lemons, mandarins, peaches, and pineapples."

The variety and splendor of the plants was astonishing, but the mention of Spanish oranges pained her. Her parents had been sailing to Spain when their ship went down. And her father particularly wanted to see the orange groves. But nothing good would come of dwelling on the past. Thus, she attempted to match his happy mood.

"No apple trees or mulberries?" she teased. "Should I be disappointed?"

"We don't waste space on them in here," the earl explained, "but we do have plenty of both on the grounds. Come see our pinery-vinery."

They strolled to an area where pineapples and grapes grew together.

"A wonder," she exclaimed.

Dotted about the orangery were white marble statues, some in alcoves, some central, some in front of small pools. There were benches and decorative tiles, too, but most of the building was taken up with healthy looking plants.

Then she heard a sound, the distinct squeaky, scratchy clucking sound of a partridge.

Patience went toward it. The bird had a green ribbon around its neck and was tied to the base of a leafless tree with spiny twiggy branches that seemed too big for its pot.

"What on earth?" But she was smiling already, before Lord Beaumont explained.

"A partridge in a pear tree. Or it is supposed to be. Blasted thing won't stay on a branch so my butler tethered it like a dog or a horse to the base."

"That pear tree doesn't live in the orangery, does it? If it does, then I think your entire magnificent heating system has been put to waste."

He shot her his crooked grin. "I directed Mr. Barnes who directed one of my gardeners to dig it up and put it in here. I didn't think the partridge would want to sit on a grapevine or an orange tree."

Patience approached the bird that was lunging to the end of its ribbon. On second thought, she decided not to try to pet its smooth feathers.

"But why?" she asked. "You went to an awful lot of trouble."

"Because, you are my guest, and it is the first day of Christmas."

She stayed quiet, but the famous old song's line played in her head—*my true love sent to me.*

"You have truly surprised me. Thank you."

"May I approach you?" Lord Beaumont asked, "or shall I call Mr. Barnes to tether you first?"

Patience didn't answer, yet neither did she tell him no. She waited as he slowly came closer, the partridge making the only sound as it strained in the other direction. That and her beating heart, which she vowed sounded like a drumbeat in her ear.

And then, inevitably, he asked, "May I kiss you?"

Why not? Patience had decided there was no harm in a kiss, as long as one was not discovered. She didn't bother to look around, knowing them to be alone.

She nodded. His mouth descended upon hers, and as she dissolved into pure sensation, the buzzing in her head drowned out even the noisy bird.

His tongue caressed the seam of her lips, which she opened for his gentle assault. Then, while she was still growing accustomed to the thrilling feelings swirling inside her, he broke the kiss.

"Now, over this way, you'll find our precious limes. They're harder to grow than lemons or oranges, so we keep the lime trees in the warmest spot."

With that, Lord Beaumont walked away as if he hadn't just kissed her until she couldn't think straight. Following him, she wordlessly accepted the lime he picked and offered, putting it to her nose for a good long sniff. The aroma was pungent, sharp, exhilarating. Then she dropped it into her pocket.

"We had best return to the manor," he said. "It won't do to dally here and have anyone thinking ill of us, would it?"

Patience's mouth opened slightly, particularly since it was Boxing Day and no one was thinking of them at all. However, since he was being responsible, she had to agree. Except for one thing.

"What about the partridge?"

The earl smiled. "I guess we must decide right now whether to set it free or give it to Cook for tomorrow's dinner."

"*Oh!*" Hungry as she often had been the past few months, she couldn't stomach the idea of eating the bird who'd played a part in her first day of Christmas. Besides, the pretty ribbon around its scrawny neck was as green as Lord Beaumont's eyes.

"I couldn't possibly eat the poor thing." She didn't mention that she had no intention of still being there at dinnertime the next day.

"Very good answer," he said. "The bird has provided a service and deserves clemency." With that, he approached the pear tree, untied the ribbon, and headed toward the exit with Patience trailing behind man and bird, who waddled quickly to keep up, jumping into the air every few feet.

"I have never held one that I haven't killed and been brought to me by one of my hunting dogs," Lord

Beaumont said when they reached the orangery door. "This could be tricky."

After handing her the end of the ribbon, he pulled his thick winter gloves from his pocket and donned them. Thus protected from the partridge's beak, he bent down and captured the bird, managing to hold with one hand upon its back while he untied the ribbon from around its neck.

"Open the door, please," he asked.

Patience did so quickly, receiving a blast of frigid air across her bare face.

Scooping up the bird, Lord Beaumont thrust it out onto the snowy path.

Instantly, the partridge erupted into flight, beating the air with quick wings. They watched its progress, flying close to the ground before it disappeared into the shrubbery. After sharing a quick satisfied smile, they retraced their footsteps to the manor.

"I hope you enjoyed the orangery, my lady. If you'll forgive me, I must allow you some free time as I have a few things to attend to in my study. Please make use of my library, or if you play, the conservatory. Do you?"

She was staring at his lips, foolishly wishing she could kiss him goodbye but knowing she was going to do something terribly drastic in the next few minutes and wouldn't see him again. Not for a while.

"Do I what?"

"Play the piano or the violin? Both are in the conservatory, although I cannot attest to how well tuned the instruments are. Do you recall how to get there?"

"Yes, thank you." She didn't tell him she was only a fair pianist and worse at the violin, nor that she would not be going to the library or to the music room.

After bowing over her hand, his lordship strode along the hallway. Patience watched him, wishing she didn't have to leave. If she weren't breaking all the rules of normalcy and civility by staying alone with him, if she weren't worrying over her estate and her small staff, if she weren't certain Lord Beaumont could charm her out of her home and into his bed, she might actually be enjoying herself.

Hurrying to her room, Patience met no one. Some servants, if their families were local, would have trudged through the snow to spend the day with them. Others who had nowhere close to go would simply have their feet up in the servants' quarters, enjoying their own treats and cups of chocolate. At least, she was counting on that.

After thrusting her evening gown into one of her bags before thinking better of it and returning it to the wardrobe along with her other day gown, she changed out of her house slippers and into her sturdy boots. With her thick, fur-lined cloak fastened and her warm hat tugged over her head, she went down to the kitchen carrying her all-but empty bags.

It didn't take her any time at all to pack them to bursting with loaves of bread, a ham in each, a pound of butter wrapped in a linen cloth, a half a round of cheese, the earthenware jar of jam with which she would surprise her staff, and as many root vegetables as she could put on top and still close the bags.

Kicking herself for not searching out the tea caddy, Patience dragged the bags out the back and along the shoveled path to the stables, while not meeting a single soul. It had been too easy. With a mixture of sadness and relief, at last, she was on her way.

CHAPTER EIGHT

Having ridden since she was a child, Patience easily saddled a sturdy mare and then had the more difficult task of securing her bounty. Using spare reins tied to the bags' handles, she looped the ends over the saddle and fastened them as tightly as she could. It took longer than she'd wished.

Setting out, Patience went down the drive, fearing she would get lost if she didn't retrace the route by which she'd arrived. With bewilderment, she soon found the snow upon the landscape changed everything. While the horse seemed game to plod along, within fifteen minutes, Patience was no longer sure she was heading in the correct direction.

"Not to worry," she said aloud to comfort herself. As soon as she saw the church spire in the distance, relief washed over her, although it wasn't exactly where she thought it would be. Moreover, she and her horse seemed to have climbed a steep hill and put a gully between her and home.

There was nothing to do but go down. The snow was deeper the farther she descended. After half an hour, the horse stopped. It had to because the snow was above its knees.

"Hells bells!" To make it worse, the sky had grown a darker shade of gray, and if she wasn't mistaken, snow was falling in the distance. A shard of fear sliced her. The plan that had seemed rational and easy a few hours earlier had taken on the aura of risk if not downright danger.

Dismounting, the snow came up to her thighs under her gown, and when she took the first step, it went over the tops of her boots and coated her stockings.

"Blast!" She needed to turn the horse and get back up the hill to where the snow was half as deep. It was a struggle just to get the mare facing the right way. Then they began a slow climb. As soon as it was easier traveling, Patience remounted, more ungracefully than she ever had in her life.

With her legs and toes cold, she contemplated her options, which were few. There was nothing to do but keep going. A half hour later, she was thoroughly lost. At least it was not dark, but the snow was falling fast, and her cloak became soaked where snowflakes landed and then melted through.

Patience staved off her burgeoning panic by singing the Snap Dragon song and imagining herself in Lord Beaumont's warm salon, sipping brandy. It had been a glorious Christmas after all.

She sniffed.

"You shall not cry like a babe!" she ordered.

When the watery winter sun disappeared over the horizon, and she was no closer to finding home nor to returning to Beaumont Manor, which she would settle for, Patience leaned over the mare's neck and bawled.

"I'm so sorry," she told the horse. "I suppose I could at least dig in the bags and find you some carrots for all your troubles."

"Russ!"

"Don't you start calling me that," Patience scolded the mare, wishing she could dry her cheeks, but her gloves were soaked, too, and her fingers were too frozen to move anyway.

"Russ!" The call drifted toward her, although the whipping snow made it hard to see more than a few yards ahead and she could not see the earl.

"Lord Beaumont," she returned, but the sound was muffled. "Come along, my girl," Patience encouraged herself. "You can yell more loudly than that."

Something shorter would suffice. "Nate!" she called. And again, "Nate! Nate! Nate!"

Like a beacon, his horse and then his tall figure in the saddle parted the snow like a curtain. He held a lantern which gave off warm, yellow light.

Her heart thumped with the knowledge she had been found. Either they would die together in the snow, or he would get them home. Regardless, she was no longer alone.

NATHANIEL HAD NEVER BEEN so frightened in his entire life, not even when he learned of the reckless race his father intended to embark upon.

Nor had he ever prayed so hard, nor felt tears well and threaten to overflow upon seeing someone. But when he caught a glimpse of Russ's blue cloak in the swirling snow, he nearly broke down with relief.

"Thank you, God in Heaven."

After determining she was not injured, he wanted only to get them home as swiftly as possible. To that end, he set her in front of him on his horse, wrapping his arms around her so they could share their body warmth.

Because he had near-perfect sense of direction and because his horse's was even better, they made it home directly, despite the worsening conditions. They had ridden in silence, leading the mare that she'd stolen.

Indoors, Russ was like a wilted flower, barely able to stand so he carried her up the stairs—*bloody backbreaking task*—and laid her on her bed. She closed her eyes and said nothing.

"Undress and get under the covers," he ordered. "I must tend to the horses. Blasted boxing day!"

As quickly as possible, Nathaniel put the two mounts safely back in the stables and deposited her bags, which he discovered were stuffed full of *his* food, in the main hallway. Then he took the stairs two at a time and knocked on her door.

With no response, he pushed it open. Russ hadn't moved.

"Why didn't you do as I told you?" he asked, frustrated.

"Too cold," she murmured, not opening her eyes.

As far as he knew, Jane wasn't on the estate and wouldn't be for another few hours. Therefore, he took it upon himself to light a fire in the hearth and draw the curtains closed. Then he stood at the foot of the bed.

"Shall I take off your boots?"

Russ nodded, then said, "I'm afraid I have no toes. No feet at all."

Christ! Nathaniel removed her boots to find her stockings soaked and cold. They would have to go as well.

"May I remove your stockings, or can you do it?"

No answer. He realized she was crying. *The devil!* A crying woman. No staff. *What next?* A snowstorm. But of course, that was already raging. Some of his servants might not make it home that night, and they'd be short-handed in the morning.

There was nothing for it but to get on with it and pretend there was nothing untoward about him pushing her skirts up and removing her hosiery. He could do it from the foot of the bed.

Parting her soaked cloak, knowing Mrs. Corely would become an ogress when she saw the mess, Nathaniel pushed her thick traveling gown up her legs. Slender, shapely legs. The petticoat and shift had to be lifted, too.

He swallowed and tugged at the ribbons holding her fine wool stockings in place a few inches above her knees.

"You should not have done what you did! An asinine adventure that nearly got you killed. Not to mention my mare. What were you thinking?"

He drew the stockings down, the first time he had done such a thing without the promise of a tupping taking place shortly after.

"And you didn't bother to say goodbye. There I was, gathering up two blasted turtle doves for tomorrow, although they're not really the turtle kind at all. None to be had this time of year. I had to settle for doves that don't migrate to warmer climates. Common wood pigeons, in fact."

By this time, he was rubbing her chilled feet between his hands to warm them and bring back some feeling. As a child, he'd played outside too long and had tried to warm his hands by plunging them into hot water, an incredibly painful experience.

"Can you feel your feet now, Russ?"

But she was still crying softly so he went back to talking. "And what were you thinking by stealing food? The only reason I searched your whereabouts was when Cook came out of the servants' quarters looking for her special pot of jam and discovering it missing. What an uproar!"

He tucked the counterpane over her feet and went to the side of the bed. Tears leaked from her closed eyes and her face was pale. *Poor thing!*

"Off with your hat," he said, getting used to taking liberties with her person. He untied the ribbon under her chin and drew it off, tossing it to the floor behind him.

"Now your wet gloves. I should have started there."

Lifting each hand, he stripped off her sodden gloves, and these joined her hat.

"Can you feel your fingers?"

No response. "Russ, would you open your lovely eyes and speak to me?"

"No," she said.

He chuckled at her stubborn single word, which alleviated some of his worry. Picking up her right hand, he began to rub it between his own. It was so soft and delicate, he again gave thanks that she was alive and back under his roof. He could easily have missed her in the storm.

"If you had taken everything else but left behind the jam, I might not have known you'd gone. In any case, it wasn't the preserves so much as Cook's favorite stoneware pot," he explained, hoping her pallor would improve. "She breached the Boxing Day etiquette and came to find me. Or maybe the rules apply only to me, as I am not supposed to disturb her or the rest of my staff."

Taking hold of her other hand, Nathaniel gave it the same treatment.

"After the jam pot incident, Cook realized two hams were missing, and that led to her discovering what all else you had stuffed in your bags."

He couldn't help laughing. "You were like old St. Nicholas instead of St. Claire, and with food rather than toys."

Realizing he'd left her skirts up, exposing her legs, he drew the layers of fabric down as respectfully as possible. After all, he would never do anything as dastardly low as taking advantage of a woman. Those who did were the lowest forms of rascals, the hell hounds with whom a more fastidious, civilized rake did not wish to be associated.

After poking the fire to give it a little air, Nathaniel returned to sit on the side of the bed.

"We should get you out of the rest of your clothing."

"No," she said again.

"It's not healthy to stay dressed in cold, damp fabric. Don't be an arse!"

Finally, her eyelids fluttered open, and he lost himself in the ocean of sadness swirling in their depths.

"Russ," he groaned. "You scared me."

Without thinking, he leaned over and claimed her mouth, a quick, hard kiss that reassured him she was *chopping,* in lusty good health. She didn't respond. Maybe her lips were too cold and numb, but he thought it was something else—whatever was making her cry.

"I scared myself," she said quietly. "But you must take me home. Immediately." Then she sighed as if she was too tired to contemplate it.

"Why?" he asked.

"Because." She closed her eyelids once more. "My people are starving."

He brushed the hair off her forehead. "They are not."

Her eyes snapped open, and their intense blue flame was back.

CHAPTER NINE

"They are!" Patience had failed, and now she was growing angry, both at herself for getting lost and at Nathaniel Beaumont for thinking he knew better.

"You cannot know the situation at St. Claire Hall. But it is a dismal one. Mr. Crawford is no driver, as you may have guessed. I didn't bring a maid because I have only one, and she slipped on the ice because there was no one to remove it off the step. My cook cannot do her job because the pantry and larder are empty. And while I have been gorging myself with you, they have had little but bread and broth."

"And you brought two empty bags to Lady Kepelton's because you intended to fill them with pilfered food."

"I know her cook. I wouldn't have had to steal," Patience explained. "More like help myself and she would turn a blind eye."

"But you stole from me rather than asking for help."

"Because you want to marry me for my land." She tossed one arm over her face to cover her eyes. "And if you knew my dire circumstances, you would convince me to marry and turn everything over to you. Then you would get me with child and go back to your licentious ways."

Silence met her words. After a moment, she peered out from under her arm. His thunderstruck expression, eyebrows raised, eyes widened, was almost comical.

"Well, you would," she insisted.

"Stay right there." His lordship rose to his feet. "No, on second thought, while I go away for a minute or two, get out of those wet clothes. If you haven't done so, I shall strip you myself when I return."

With that daunting threat, he stormed from the room.

Taking him at his word, although having him play lady's maid would be interesting and torturously exciting, Patience got out of bed. Her feet hurt. Her hands hurt. Her head throbbed. She was lightheaded and all-overish out of sorts. Yet she quickly took off her gown and lay it over the tufted chair. Her petticoat came next and then her corset.

However, beneath it all, her shift was dry, so she climbed back onto the sinfully comfortable down mattress and pulled the bed linens up over her chest for modesty's sake, belated though that might be.

When his hands had skimmed her bare legs while removing her stockings, she thought it the most sensual thing in the world. But she was too distraught to have enjoyed it properly.

The door opened without the earl knocking. Lord Beaumont—whom more and more, especially since he'd rubbed her feet, she was thinking of as Nathaniel—entered carrying two glasses, each half full of amber liquid.

"Good. You took me seriously," he said upon seeing her clothes over the chair. "Although I would have enjoyed undressing you."

Patience didn't bother being shocked. She merely took the brandy he proffered. Then the earl took up a position leaning against the bed post.

"Why were you crying earlier? Feeling sorry for yourself, were you?"

"I was not," she said. "I was thinking of having failed my very tiny staff of three."

"Then I want you to cheer up," he said. "The first day you came, I spoke with a groom named Oliver Bell. Do you know him?"

"I do. He was employed as my driver until two months ago yet worked as a groom before my former driver left. Thus, Mr. Crawford is my third driver, and he is not really much good at all."

She was blathering, feeling anxious. *Why had he spoken with Oliver?*

"When asked, Mr. Bell told me the state of affairs at St. Claire Hall."

Patience nearly spilled the brandy as she sat up quickly. "He had no right to do that. It is disloyal. Treasonous!"

"Calm your feathers, my lady. He spoke frankly because I offered to help. And because he still has friends at St. Claire Hall. I sent food in the sledge within an hour of speaking with him."

Patience knew her mouth had dropped open because she had to close it. Then she took another sip of brandy and relaxed against the pillows.

It was galling and humiliating, but the ends justified the means, as they said. Knowing Cook and Eliza and Mr. Crawford weren't hungry settled over her like a warm blanket.

"I am greatly relieved. Why didn't you tell me?"

"I did not wish to embarrass you," Nathaniel said. "I was waiting for you to speak as frankly to me as Mr. Bell did. I never conceived of your stealing my horse and food and slipping away into a blizzard."

"It was not snowing when I left, and I wouldn't have kept the mare." She rolled her eyes. "I certainly do not need another mouth to feed."

"Tell me how you got into your current dilemma."

Patience didn't want to bore him with the long slow decline of the estate. As succinctly as possible, she told him how the income had dwindled in the months after her parents died. Moreover, she had no idea why, nor how to increase it to its previous levels. She knew nothing of investing or purchasing or precisely how to run what she had inherited. She had merely the name of a lawyer in London, and he had been of little help.

"I was only able to keep the Hall because there were no male heirs in sight. Not even an uncle or long-forgotten cousin. I certainly couldn't have foretold I would ever be in charge. My parents must have assumed the man I married would handle the estate once they passed away. No one could have anticipated such a catastrophe *before* I married."

"Which brings us to you and me," Lord Beaumont said."

"Does it?" She ignored the obvious. He was going to press his advantage. He knew her secrets, he had her under his roof unchaperoned, and he was ready to swoop in and claim her hand and her estate. She'd been right to keep him at a distance, and Lady Priscilla had spoken the truth.

Sipping her brandy, Patience waited.

"You leveled some severe and damning accusations regarding how I might behave should we form a marital union," Nathaniel said, surprising her. "On what do you base these claims?"

He looked as if his drawers were in a twist—quite out of sorts. Patience hiccupped before answering.

"Do you deny your reputation?"

"I do not deny having made some females very happy."

He had certainly made *her* happy with skillful kisses and a few tantalizing caresses. Patience could scarcely imagine how happy other acts might make her.

"You enjoy the company of women," she said carefully. "And *after* marriage, then what?"

"I intend to marry a woman, so I shall continue to enjoy female companionship."

He was dodging the issue. "You know what I meant. Will you be faithful to your wife? To the *company* of one woman?"

"I will," he said, his tone serious. "I shall be enchanted and enamored with the woman whose hand I take in wedlock. Why marry otherwise?"

Hm. That was the crux of the matter.

Patience spoke plainly. "For an estate, perhaps."

"Who filled your head with such rubbish?" he demanded.

"A year ago at Lady Kepelton's party, Lady Priscilla Malcolm Price said you were after my estate."

"Absurd. Did you think to ask me?"

"No. If it was true, you would deny it. If it was false, you would deny it." Patience had been dismayed that Lady Priscilla knew she and Nathaniel were forming an attachment. Dismay had become shock when she'd heard the lady's prediction of what might occur.

"Besides, Lady Priscilla seemed to know of what she spoke, as if she had first-hand knowledge, hearing it from your own lips."

Nathaniel shook his head. "Then she either misunderstood something I said, or she willfully and boldly lied."

Patience considered that. "Why would Lady Priscilla do such a thing?"

He stared at her, and she could almost feel a dunce cap growing atop her head.

"Have you looked at her?" the earl asked. "I mean, really looked at her?"

Patience frowned. "Yes, of course."

He huffed and drained his glass. "She reminds me of nothing so much as my favorite horse, Bayard. The one which rescued you today, in fact."

"That's a terrible thing to say," Patience admonished him.

"You are right, Russ. And as soon as I see my horse again, I'll apologize and take him a carrot from Cook's precious root cellar."

With that, he stormed across the room to set his empty glass on the dressing table.

Patience thought about what Nathaniel had said, and then, rather wickedly, she began to laugh. It wasn't that Lady Priscilla had such a very long face. It was the way she flared her nostrils and moved her upper lip when she spoke, like a horse whinnying.

Suddenly, all she could think of was the lady holding a steel bit in her mouth. Once Patience started laughing, she could not stop.

The earl stomped back toward her. Before she could say anything, he made the route again. Pacing, he was also muttering to himself about her and Priscilla and females in general.

Finally, he stopped at the end of the bed, one hand curled around a carved post.

"An absurd thing for her to say and even more ridiculous for you to believe," he railed. "I do *not* need St. Claire Hall, nor do I want it. What would I do with that crumbling residence?"

"St. Claire Hall isn't crumbling. At least, it wasn't, not a year ago."

"When Lady Priscilla spoke her poison in your ear and turned you against me, did you bother to recall the kisses we'd shared only hours earlier? And the day before?"

Patience lifted her chin. "You have shared similar with many a lady, as we have recently gone over."

"*Argh!*" he roared. "What about the discourse we partook of, seeming to be like-minded and in the most advantageous harmony?"

She shrugged. "How could I know that wasn't an act as well-performed as any who walk the stage in London?"

He blinked. "I must ask you the same as I asked about Lady Priscilla. Have you seen yourself in the looking glass?"

While flattered, appearances were not everything. "A fair face is not enough to secure a man's heart *or* his fidelity, at least not in the long run," she protested.

"You did not give me a chance to explore what more there might have been between us. What of my spurned gifts and visits to St. Claire Hall?"

What could she say? Patience had never truly supposed a worldly man of his stature would or could fall for her.

"I may have let Lady Priscilla scare me away from giving you an opportunity," she said primly.

With his ire raised, Nathaniel rumped her quite spectacularly, with a flick of his dark gray coat for emphasis. Muttering to himself, he crossed the room, speaking just loudly enough for her to hear.

"As if I would marry someone for their ugly house! How ludicrous! Doesn't the chit know I can have any woman I please?"

By that time, he was at the bedroom door. "I am going to release the pigeons." Then he slammed it in his wake.

When he returned an hour later, Patience had risen to relieve herself and to stoke the fire. Other than that, she hadn't felt the strength to dress in her other gown and go downstairs.

This time, he knocked softly before sticking his head around the door.

"Are you awake? I've brought you some nourishment."

Her head swam, and she didn't feel well at all. However, seeing how it was all her own fault, she made the effort to sit up and lean back upon the headboard. Not really hungry, regardless, she knew she ought to eat, if for no other reason than to be polite.

"Simple fare from my own hand," Nathaniel said, sounding proud before setting a plate on her lap.

Ham, bread, and cheese. Probably from her bags since she doubted he had any idea where to find food in his own kitchen.

"Yes," he admitted. "I emptied your ill-gotten gains onto the kitchen table and found it to be just what I fancied."

Nodding, she picked up a heel of bread and looked at him, directly into his jade-colored eyes. "I didn't yet thank you for coming after me. Or for sending food to the Hall. Thus, let me tell you now, I am exceedingly grateful."

Then, because her throat felt dry, she asked, "Could I have some water, please?"

His expression altered, and without asking, he put the back of his hand to her forehead, startling her.

"You're warm."

"Finally, yes," she agreed. "Toasty."

"You don't feel *too* warm, do you? Or chilled?"

"Simply thirsty."

"Of course." Like a tardy chamber maid, he bounded from the room, returning two minutes later with a wineglass of water.

"I couldn't find another glass. It was that or a steel tankard with my family's coat of arms."

"This will do nicely," she said, draining the glass.

"Shall I send for the physician?"

Shaking her head, Patience handed him the empty goblet. "I shall be right as rain in no time. I'll eat this and then manage to rouse myself and join you downstairs. It must be strangely quiet without any of your staff milling about. You shall be sick of the sight of me soon, I warrant."

CHAPTER TEN

Nathaniel was *not* sick of her. Quite the contrary. Russ was the one who fell ill.

After waiting for her to come downstairs, he went a third time to her bedchamber. She had set aside her plate with most of the food untouched upon it. Having kicked off the bed linens, she lay shivering, eyes closed, and curled upon her side.

After a silent oath, he quickly covered her and added another blanket from the linen chest against the wall. Then he stoked the fire and . . . felt helpless. Utterly useless. He didn't need to touch her forehead again to see she was feverish.

His mother had cared for both him and his sister through various ailments and would have known what to do. There was nothing for it but to venture into the servants' quarters and ask for assistance.

To his surprise, despite having her day off interrupted, his fearsome housekeeper leapt into action.

"Peppermint oil for a chest poultice and barley water," Mrs. Corely demanded of her staff. To the cook, she said,

"A cup of warm broth, preferably chicken or duck, but beef will do in a pinch."

"I'll get the invalid's cup," she added, referring to the silver handled cup Nathaniel hadn't seen since childhood, with a spout on one side that could be put directly into the sick person's mouth.

"Perhaps some powdered rhubarb root," Cook offered on her way out.

"It wouldn't hurt to try," Mrs. Corely said.

It was probably ghastly, Nathaniel thought. But he let the women have full and free rein.

"If she's able," said his butler, "a mustard bath might help?"

"You have gone too far, Mr. Barnes," Mrs. Corely said. "If the lady's abed with a fever, as his lordship says, then *no* bath. Not till she's up and about."

Nathaniel liked hearing that his housekeeper didn't doubt Russ would be on her feet again at some point.

"I've got some willow bark," Mr. Barnes tried again. "I keep it for my aches, but I have it on good authority it works well for ague, too."

Nathaniel hadn't realized his butler ached. But since the man was twenty years older than him if he was a day, he ought to have assumed such.

"I thought you were going into the village," Nathaniel said.

"I couldn't be bothered, my lord," Mr. Barnes replied. "Not with the weather. Seemed a fool's endeavor."

Nathaniel agreed wholeheartedly, but his butler shouldn't have said it, seeing how at least a third of the staff had ventured out.

"Jane is one of the fool's," Mrs. Corely said, having picked up on the conversation, "so I shall tend to the lady myself. And I'll take that willow bark, Mr. Barnes."

"Thank you," Nathaniel said, feeling a lump in his throat. "Both of you. I'm very grateful."

"Yes, my lord." With that, his housekeeper followed his cook out of the room.

"I shall retrieve the powdered willow bark, my lord," said Mr. Barnes. He bowed and went down the hall to his small room.

"Thank you," Nathaniel called after him.

And what could *he* do to help? Nothing. He made his way back to his study, only to recall the pigeons. After planning on releasing the birds earlier, Nathaniel had discovered they'd escaped the basket in which he'd placed them and were flying around the room. Having decided to deal with them later, the situation with Russ had entirely distracted him.

What a mess! Droppings were all over his desk, chair, and carpet. And no useful chambermaid to come clean it up. The pigeons cooed at him from their perch on the top shelf of his bookcase.

Nathaniel spent a quarter of an hour catching them, all the while considering whether he ought to get his hunting rifle to speed up the process.

In the end, he'd been reduced to throwing his jacket over each in turn and putting it outside. To the second one, as he released it, he said, "You are fortunate we're not having you in a pie."

He simply didn't fancy eating what he had intended to present to the lady. It seemed unfair and bad luck to boot.

LADY PATIENCE MISSED THE next few days of the Twelvetide, remaining in a "moderate fever," as Mrs. Corely called it.

Thus, Nathaniel didn't have to bother with three French hens. He had intended to spray two of Cook's regular hens with some French perfume his mother had left behind. As for the colly birds, various blackbirds abounded on his property, and he would have had no trouble rounding up four of them.

When it came to the five gold rings, he would have gladly given a king's ransom if Russ would appear in the drawing room, hale and saucy.

While she recovered, he sent word to St. Claire Hall, telling her minimal staff what had happened, along with giving them another delivery of food. He asked that they send back a trunk of their lady's clothing, which they did.

"I think Lady Patience was exhausted," Jane said. The maid had remained at Russ's bedside since her return from the village on Boxing Day. "Her constitution was weak, if you ask me, milord, from running her own home and the Christmas party and then the way you let her ride off on her own, begging your pardon, my lord."

"You heard about that, did you?" Nathaniel had confided in his butler and housekeeper about the circumstances leading up to Russ's collapse.

"Oh, yes," Jane said cheerfully. "We *all* did. 'Neglect begets disaster.' That's what Mrs. Corely says."

Neglect? It had hardly been that.

"Hopefully, disaster has been averted," Nathaniel said. "Aren't you supposed to be somewhere, Jane?" He'd run into her in the main hallway, and she was making him feel worse.

"Oh, yes," she repeated. "Mrs. Corely thinks Lady Patience might be ready for slipslops." Then she made a face. "Watery gruel, milord."

"I know what it is." He probably wore a similar expression of dislike. He'd been force-fed it once or twice as a child.

"Her ladyship was very thin when she got here," Jane added. "If we don't fatten her up, she'll disappear altogether by Twelfth Night."

What a dreadful thing to say!

Returning to his study, Nathaniel busied himself reading and answering correspondence, although he had yet to receive a return letter from London. Regardless, he had confidence his shrewd lawyer would suss out whether there was any way to assist Russ in handling St. Claire Hall.

And then he spent the day alone, missing her company more than he thought possible. It wasn't as though she'd been with him for weeks, and yet he keenly felt her absence at dinner and afterward.

"Foolishness," Nathaniel said aloud before settling down with a book in the small salon where they had played Snap Dragon.

Pouring himself a glass of brandy, he attributed his moroseness to being in the country when he ought to be in London where every amusement in the world was offered to a gentleman of means. What's more, the manor was unusually empty, not having his mother, the Dowager Lady Beaumont, in residence. They often played cards or draughts in the evenings when they weren't entertaining his or her friends.

His mother would like Russ. Nathaniel was sure of it. He certainly liked her. *A great deal!* Even more now that he knew it had been the interference of that horse-faced Lady Priscilla who'd muddied the waters.

Of course, his own less-than-pure reputation had played a part. He considered Russ's fears and discarded them. He could and would be a faithful husband. After all, he felt more than lust for her already. Hadn't he tried more than once to pay a polite call in order to request the honor of courting her?

When he returned to London last spring, he had compared every other woman he kissed to her—and found them lacking. Somehow, she had made an indelible mark upon him, perhaps in the region of his heart.

It would be easy to fall completely in love with her if he wasn't already.

Sighing, he hoped she would be back on her pretty slippered feet by the time they reached the drummers drumming.

As it turned out, he didn't have to wait that long. On the first day of the new year, Russ appeared at the breakfast table. He jumped to his feet so quickly, he knocked the table and spilled his chocolate onto the table linen.

Not thinking of the propriety of his actions, he rushed forward and took hold of her hands, both of them.

"You are here!" An idiotic utterance. "You look much improved." That was better said. "I am so pleased to see you." Finally, the truth. "I have sorely missed you and asked my staff every hour as to your well-being."

Russ smiled, and his heart ached. Yes, indeed. The lady had deeply impacted his sensibilities. Nathaniel nearly kissed her before restraining himself and instead drew out a chair for her.

"Thank you," she said. "I am pleased to see you again, as well. Your staff must have willed me to good health in order to cease your bothersome queries."

He laughed. "And they have done a grand job of it. You have a healthy glow to your cheeks. Jane said all we need do is fatten you up."

Her eyes widened. "Like a goose before the Christmas feast?"

"Precisely. Let us begin with a large breakfast."

He loaded her plate with everything, hoping he could ensure she never went hungry again.

"Speaking of geese," he said, resuming his seat, "I had no luck finding a single one that was laying an egg yesterday, never mind six of them, or I would have brought them to your room." Nathaniel could barely believe how happy her presence made him.

"Then I am glad you didn't find any," Russ said. "They are noisy and fearsome birds. What about seven swans? Any luck?"

"Luck!" he scoffed. "The Beaumont family purchased a mark granting us swan ownership since the late sixteen hundreds."

"Impressive!" She sounded as though she meant it and understood the prestige and expense of owning such an honor.

"Our mark is like a sideways sail with two dashes on the beak. We have easily a dozen of the non-migratory swans. Alas, when the pond closest to the house froze, they moved to a nearby lake. My groundskeeper shall fetch them back in the spring."

"So no swans until then," she teased him. "A pity."

"Just you wait, Russ, until dinner."

She gasped. "No, my lord. They must be swimming. I vow I shall *not* eat one. They are too beautiful."

He laughed at her expression. "It may have sounded like I meant to serve you one, plucked and roasted. The bird, not me. Yet I assure you, I did not intend any such thing. Again, you must wait and see."

"I am afraid that waiting is all I shall be doing. Despite spending longer resting than I have before in my life, any undertaking seems too great, even needlepoint."

"Needlepoint would be my last choice," Nathaniel agreed, "far below doing nothing. Perhaps you would enjoy reading a novel. I own some good ones."

She brightened, and he was thrilled.

"Yes," she said. "I never made it to your library, since I was too busy stealing your food, but I would relish choosing a book."

CHAPTER ELEVEN

An hour before dinner, Patience felt a flutter of anticipatory nervousness. She had whiled away the long hours of the day doing as Nathaniel had suggested, reading in a cozy chair before the fire.

At one point, she stretched her legs, taking a slow walk by herself through the manor's galleries. The earl had been correct in stating she'd moved too quickly when he'd given her a tour the day she arrived. She had missed a great deal of interesting paintings and some busts, too.

Nathaniel came to find her once and share a cup of tea in the library, but otherwise, he'd had business to which he attended in his study. It reminded her how her father used to devote a measure of his day to the estate's accounts and its management.

How would she keep her birthright? That question floated about her mind while she watched him leave, a devilishly handsome man. She sighed, no longer able to keep her mind on *Crotchet Castle,* an anonymous work that wasn't really about a castle at all. A cruel trick of the title. Moreover it was too much blathering without any purpose.

Placing it on the table beside Mrs. Gore's *Pin Money*, which she had thought far more engaging, she considered her future. She wasn't a ninny, after all. She ought to delve into the accounts and not rely on the London lawyer to tell her what was what.

The problem was that she had neither an interest in such things, nor a head for numbers. They always seemed to squiggle and move around and not make sense, especially when they were in columns on a ledger. She would rather paint a picture or ride a horse or even raise children, for that matter.

In truth, Patience had never wished to take up the mantle of estate manager, nor could she afford to hire one. However, she could ask Lord Beaumont for his advice, if only she was certain he wouldn't see it as a sign of weakness.

He had called St. Claire Hall crumbling and said he didn't "need" it, but what if he *wanted* it? Worse, what if he wanted it more than he wanted her?

At dinner, she wore a dress from home. In a navy-blue gown of the finest wool, accented with delicate cream-colored lace at the neckline and at the ends of her sleeves, softening its appearance, she felt confident. Nathaniel's appreciative gaze rewarded her effort. And it *had* been an effort to change and allow Jane to dress her hair. It took every last ounce of strength not to collapse back onto the four-poster bed.

But she hadn't.

"It is delightful to see you at the end of the day," Nathaniel confessed, echoing her thoughts.

Although theirs was a temporary situation, it seemed to be good practice for the pattern of a blissful marriage. Coming together and moving apart and coming together again over the course of a day.

"Now that you know your staff is being fed, will you agree to stay until Advent?"

Patience was glad he had asked. She'd spent more time convalescing in the blue room than she had with him. And as he'd said, her staff was taken care of, so what harm could there be in remaining at the manor? She could hide from her problems a little longer.

"I would like to stay," she admitted. After all, if anyone cared to look into the matter, her reputation would already be in ruins.

"Perhaps we should throw a Twelfth Night ball," he said. "Again we could do so as neighboring hosts. If you feel up to it, of course. Maybe it is too soon. I just thought that we have hardly celebrated the Twelvetide."

She discounted his concern over her health with a wave of her hand. After all, she would have four days to rest.

"Would the ball be for the villagers?" Patience imagined the cider maker trying to dance a waltz.

"Actually," Nathaniel said, "I was thinking of those who might not have enjoyed any festivities due to Lady Kepelton's cancelled party. People from London, I mean. As long as it doesn't snow again."

Ah, now she understood. A fashionable ball, not a party for the villagers. Her first thought was that she would love to dance with him. Her second was she hoped he did not invite Lady Priscilla.

"If you think there is time to arrange for such a thing," she agreed, "then I shall do what I can to help." Nevertheless, the ramifications had to be considered. "I believe the *ton* will make assumptions."

"Assumptions?" he asked, fiddling with his as-yet unused dessert spoon. But he had to know what she meant.

"Yes. About *us.* They will think we have an understanding."

Instead of offering an opinion, Nathaniel gestured to the footman.

"Please tell Cook we're ready for the seventh day of Christmas."

"Yes, milord."

Patience started to smile. "What mysterious surprise have you planned?"

"You will see, Russ."

"You must not call me that."

"Too late," he quipped.

The door opened and in came the same footman staggering under the weight of a large tureen, which he set down in the middle of the table.

Patience marveled at the design. In a frothy lake which she guessed to be syllabub—one of her favorite things in the whole world—seven miniature white swans were "swimming."

"What are they made out of?" she asked. Then she clapped her hands. "They are meringue! How clever."

"Cook outdid herself. I wasn't expecting such well-formed swans," Nathaniel said.

"With orange beaks and black eyes. They're perfect." She looked at the earl. "Thank you for this gift!"

When he grinned at her, looking smugly satisfied, her insides fluttered, and she wished the footman hadn't spent the entire meal standing by the sideboard, anticipating their every need. For her need at that moment was to lean over and kiss the Earl of Beaumont.

All she could do was wait while the footman ladled the syllabub and a regal swan into a bowl for her before doing the same for his lordship.

"My favorite so far," Nathaniel said. "Far better than the hens which smelled like my mother."

"I beg your pardon?" she asked.

"Never mind. Taste and enjoy," he invited.

And she did. She ate every last morsel of the sweet baked meringue before spooning the syllabub.

"That shall be my new favorite Twelvetide tradition," she vowed.

"Speaking of which, we must inspect the yule log." Nathaniel rose and offered his hand. Placing her fingers lightly on his overturned palm, she would swear a little jolt of heat went up her arm at the innocent touch. They strolled into the great room.

It looked much the same as before she fell ill, with a decorated tree at one end and the now-smaller yule log lying half-in, half-out of the massive fireplace.

"Isn't it supposed to be continuously smoldering?" she asked. "To do with good fortune or moving the sun in the sky?"

They laughed. "I don't know how those Vikings kept a log lit for twelve blasted days," Nathaniel said, using a candle from a wall sconce to set the wood burning again. "But at Beaumont Manor, we simply relight it each night. And regardless of such a blasphemy, we seem to fare perfectly well throughout the year. I would go so far as to say that we are a lucky family, apart from my father's careless demise. Regarding the sun, I have no doubt it will continue its journey and start to set later each evening, with or without a perpetually lit yule log in our particular hearth."

"I am greatly relieved," Patience said, mockingly.

Taking a walk around the tree, she looked at what was left on its branches. "The villagers enjoyed the pennies and such."

"Did your parents ever host them?" the earl asked, coming to stand beside her.

The air between them crackled. Hidden from the doorway, and any passing servants, she stared up at him, seeing a flicker of something sensual in his emerald gaze.

What was his question? Before she could answer, he set his hands upon her waist and squeezed.

"Jane is right," he said softly. "You are too thin. I could wrap my arms around you and break you like one of Cook's delicious gingersnaps."

"Please don't," Patience said.

"Or I could kiss you because I've missed your lips these past five days."

"Please do," she said.

In a heartbeat, she found herself drawn into his embrace, her breasts crushed to his chest. And then he lowered his mouth to hers. All the rest of her thoughts vanished at the familiarity of him, at his spicy fragrance, his smooth, firm lips, his wicked tongue.

Her body appreciated his touch by flaring to life as the yule log had done. The kiss continued until he rested his forehead against hers.

"Were you sniffing me, Russ?"

"No, I don't believe so. I was merely breathing. Through my nose. One must breathe, even when kissing, mustn't one?"

He nodded, not lifting his head. His hands were roaming down her back to finally rest upon her rear end, making her gasp. Suddenly, she had plenty of breath, and her heart was racing.

When he tilted her hips so she could feel his hard arousal, her temperature soared from normal to feverish again. Yet this time, she was certain she wasn't ill. If he went further, she would not protest.

Her personal boundaries had shifted and the rules of propriety seemed less important than they had a week earlier. No one in the entire world seemed to mind that she was staying without a chaperone in the Earl of Beaumont's house, nor that she was enjoying his kisses.

As with the yule log's relative unimportance in the universal truths, so too could one nobleman's daughter behave in an indecorous fashion with a disreputable earl without the sun falling from the sky.

"I look forward to the rest of the Twelvetide with you," Nathaniel said. "But we had best find a more mundane amusement to occupy ourselves, perhaps a game of draughts. Elsewise, if you continue to look at me like that, you shall find yourself well and truly compromised."

Patience deemed herself ready to be thusly compromised, imagining it would mean finally gaining relief from the longing she felt. She knew about *the act* undertaken by men and women, and that it could occur as easily out of wedlock as within. Moreover, she couldn't envision wanting to do such a thing with anyone else but Nathaniel Beaumont.

Strange that *he* was the one with the reputation for being a rake, yet *she* was the one aching between her legs and wishing he would do something about it. But she couldn't ask, so she took his arm and let him lead her to the drawing room where they played chess and then cards. Afterward, they enjoyed a light supper of pottage and toasted bread and cheese.

When she retired to her room exhausted, Patience had a feeling their connection was going to result in an engagement. His interest in her was, she'd decided, greater than any desire he might have to add her neighboring land to his estate.

"DRAW UP A MARRIAGE contract," Nathaniel wrote to his lawyer, Mr. Sudbury, in London, "with all favorable terms for Lady Patience St. Claire." He listed a generous allowance and indicated that the St. Claire estate would remain under her control to do with as she wished *after* he restored it to its former solvency.

Hopeful that he could discover some way to turn around its fortunes and thus have an extra property for their children, should they be so blessed, Nathaniel toasted his forward thinking with a glass of brandy.

The letter should reach London the following day by noon if his footman rode out early enough in the morning.

And his lawyer would be at Beaumont Manor the day after before dinnertime because no one said no to an earl.

CHAPTER TWELVE

"Are you happy here?" Patience asked the maid. They were closeted together in the blue bedchamber, as she changed out of her riding clothes.

"Oh, yes, milady. Very much so." Then Jane froze. "Have I done wrong?"

"No, not at all," Patience reassured her. But she was intent on doing a little truth-gathering. "Lord Beaumont is a kind employer, then?"

"Yes, milady."

Patience cleared her throat. "Do many ladies visit the manor?"

"I'm not sure what you mean," Jane replied. "Often the Dowager Lady Beaumont is in residence. She has many ladies who come to visit, and they often stay a week."

That told Patience nothing of what she wished to know, although it was more likely, if Nathaniel entertained any bobtails or jades, it would be at his London townhouse. Local lightskirts probably stayed in the village tavern, where he, along with any number of travelers, could visit them.

Would he? Did he? She shuddered at the notion.

Jane gave an encouraging smile. "Lord Beaumont is a fair man, milady. I've never heard him raise his voice, not even when the youngest stable boy let the new colt into Cook's garden. It was a disaster. Cook blistered the boy's ears, mind you. But not his lordship."

Jane finished tying the ribbons up the back of Patience's dress, then added, "And though I haven't been to the Beaumont home in Town, some of the servants here have. They say it's ever so plush. His lordship keeps a fine table while in London and hosts plenty of parties."

Patience nodded. She had no idea if that was a good thing or whether he invited his many lady friends over and let them host with him. Possibly when all the guests left, and it was only the two of them—

"All done, milady. And don't you look a pretty sight."

"Thank you, Jane."

Patience had spent another pleasant morning at Beaumont Manor, feeling much improved over the day before. After breakfast, Nathaniel had invited her to take a short ride around the property since the sun was shining brightly. The earl adored riding—*fast*, as it turned out, his verdant eyes sparkling like the Lord of Misrule high atop Bayard whenever the path was clear enough to gallop.

She rode a different horse from the one she'd borrowed, a spirited mount that willingly trailed behind but kept pace. Patience enjoyed herself immensely.

Now, dressed in a pleated wool day dress in a soft shade of russet and clearly meeting with Jane's approval, she left her room to find Nathaniel. Having heard the commotion of a team of horses drawing a sledge across the drive while she was changing, she went to the drawing room to meet the visitor and then to the smaller salon. Both were empty.

Hoping Nathaniel didn't mind, she strolled along the hallway toward the earl's study. The door was open, and Nathaniel's voice carried out.

"I need to know the best and the worst of St. Claire Hall and the entire estate."

"I understand, my lord," replied a voice she did not recognize. "I have done due diligence and hope you will find the information to be useful, albeit alarming. But should you not simply speak with the lady?"

She held her breath for the answer.

"No," came Nathaniel's crushing reply. "With both her parents' deceased, this is a tricky situation. And I believe I must take the entire estate under my control in order to make the necessary changes. As my wife, Lady Patience will go along with my wishes. However, at this juncture, I would rather keep her in the dark about my intent and what you have discovered."

Patience backed away silently and then hurried to her bedroom. *What to do?* She wasn't stupid enough to try to sneak away again, although she did, in fact, intend to leave as soon as she possibly could.

Lady Priscilla had been correct about Lord Beaumont's desires. And Patience would have to be on her guard to avoid the earl's smooth-as-silk, sweet-as-honey persuasion.

An hour later, Jane tapped on the door.

"His lordship is looking for you, milady. Will you join him in the conservatory?"

"The conservatory?"

"Yes, milady. That's what Lord Beaumont told me to tell you. Do you recall how to reach it?"

Patience nodded, rose from the chair where she had done nothing but stare out the window and think about Nathaniel's words. And then she went downstairs. The sounds of the elegant pianoforte reached her as she approached.

Entering, she was surprised to see Nathaniel on the leather, padded stool. He was in profile as the instrument was set before the large windows overlooking the side garden.

The music was a lilting melody, which he continued to play after glancing up and acknowledging her presence with both a nod and a smile. She went closer while he played, read the sheet music—*Sonata No. 11*—and then directed her steps toward the tufted purple velvet sofa at the other end of the pianoforte.

All the while, her insides were as jumpy as frogs, a feeling she detested.

When he completed the piece, he looked over at her. She ought to clap, but she was not in the mood to offer him even the smallest compliment.

"I did not realize you played."

Rising, he came over and sat beside her, seeming not to notice when she scooted over so their shoulders, legs, and hips did not touch.

"There are probably any number of things about me that you do not know."

A short bark of laughter escaped her. "Of that, I am certain, my lord."

He frowned slightly, perhaps at her tone.

"I believe I asked you before whether you played either the piano or," he gestured his head toward the far wall, "the violin."

She spied an open case on a table.

"I play piano," Patience told him, wondering how she could calmy get through such prattle when her heart was breaking. "I concede you to be a better musician. I am sure you are a better actor, too."

He shrugged. "Can you imagine the *ton* if an earl took to the stage? But I do like charades. When there are more than two of us, we must play."

"*Mm,*" she said noncommittally, for she intended to be home before any such occasion arose.

With his green gaze fixed upon hers, he took hold of her right hand, clasping it between his own. Those large, warm hands that had a skilled touch with the pianoforte keys and probably far more so with a woman's body.

"You wished to see me," she said, while at the same time, gently withdrawing from his grasp.

A puzzled expression crossed his face. "The staff will not bother us," he said.

"Is that so?" she asked. "Did you arrange it that way? Did you inform them that you had a plan involving me and that they must leave you to it?"

The devil grinned at her with his lopsided smile. "Yes, although not precisely those words."

"Why?" she asked. "And what of your guest?"

His eyebrows rose slightly. "You shall meet him later. I wished to ask you a question of import and for that, we needed to be alone. I know we have not known one another very long, but we have known *of* each other for quite some time. And our families are not strangers."

"*I* am my only family now," she pointed out.

"I know." He reached up and stroked her cheek with the back of his knuckles.

Patience remained still and stiff until he dropped his hand.

"While some may consider me premature in my intent, I think we are of similar minds. What's more, I believe us to be immensely compatible in every manner."

"I see." Patience took a long, steadying breath. Nathaniel was going to propose. An hour ago, she would have accepted with a full and happy heart.

"Do you?" he quipped with a tilt of his head. "You seem unlike yourself, a little crabby. Perhaps you are still feeling the consequences of your adventure. I hope our ride wasn't too soon."

"On the contrary, I am in perfect health. If you have something to say—or ask—I suggest you get on with it." She was looking forward to the end of this farce. With utter dread.

He frowned at her tone, but then he smiled. "A touch of nerves, perhaps. Very well, Lady Patience St. Claire, will you do me the honor of becoming my wife, my countess, Lady Beaumont?"

She did not hesitate to respond. "Not if you were the last man in England."

His countenance froze. "I beg your pardon?"

"I am saying *no*, my lord. I am turning you down, the equivalent of a verbal rumping. If I had a mitten at hand, I would give it to you. Do you understand me now?"

With eyes widened in confusion, Nathaniel asked, "But why? I truly thought we were forming an attachment of both mind and . . . heart."

"You thought wrong, my lord. You have carelessly made plans without regard for *my* heart."

He looked momentarily relieved. "Dearest lady, I have not forgotten it. I simply had not yet the chance to speak of such matters." He paused and tried to take her hand again, but she held it firmly in her lap.

Regardless, he continued, "My heart has grown a great fondness." He stopped, swallowed loudly, and began again. "Nay, that is too tepid a word. I thought myself merely fond of you, but I can now tell you what I feel is love."

"Love," she shot back. "Are you sure you understand the word? After all, your father was a rogue. What kind of man jeopardizes being with his wife and children to win a horserace? If he had been called to war and defense of country, that would be one thing. But he had a selfish heart. I sincerely hope your mother didn't ache for him too long. As for you, they say the apple doesn't fall far from the tree."

Stunned, he drew back. "Russ, you sound so unlike yourself. If I didn't watch your mouth speaking the words, I would vow they did not come from you. I promise you that my heart is full of effusive emotion, and it is all for you."

"A pity then," she said, rising to her feet, causing him to stand beside her. "A very great pity, for I do not return the sentiment."

"Oh!" he uttered. "I . . . that is, I am surprised." His tone was so small and, dare she say, sad that Patience nearly confessed her true feelings. But he wanted her for St. Claire. She had heard it from his own wicked lips.

"I know you have some affection for me," he said. "Each time we kiss, it is apparent."

She shrugged as if he was mistaken. "Believe what you will."

He hesitated, then said, "While I am discouraged, I am not easily dissuaded because of how much I have enjoyed your company. Thus, if you will allow it, I promise you, Russ, I will spend every day wooing you, courting you, urging you to fall in love with me until you have done so."

Patience laughed, hating the brittle sound. "That is an arrogant statement. If I haven't yet grown a *tendre* for you, then I shall not. I enjoyed the Christmas party and eating well for a change, but I am ready to return to my home. Either now, or if it is too late to set out today, then first thing in the morning. The weather is cooperating, is it not?"

He dropped his gaze to the floor. "Indeed, it is. However, it would be safer for you to start out in the morning."

"As you wish," she said. "Naturally, now that you have asked and I have turned you down, it would be impossible for me to play the hostess at your Twelfth Night ball. I shall not attend."

He nodded.

"Are we finished here?" she asked. "Or was there anything else you wished to say before you return to your music practice?"

"No, nothing." His tone, like his expression, had lost all vigor.

Patience walked away, her knees trembling, with her only desire being to reach her room before she began to cry. *How could he be so thoroughly false?* It made her doubt her ability to discern anyone's true character.

"I will see you at dinner," he called after her.

"I think not," she said without turning. She would have a plate brought to her room, and for her breakfast, too. With any luck, she needn't lay eyes upon him again.

In the hallway, she surprised eight giggling maids, all dressed alike.

Jane was one of them. "Oh, milady! You aren't supposed to be out here. We was to wait for the music to start and come in to do our pantomime."

Patience shook her head in confusion, and then it dawned on her when she saw the eight pails at their feet.

On the eighth day of Christmas my true love sent to me eight maids a milking.

The tears began to flow, and Patience ran away, with their startled exclamations following behind her.

CHAPTER THIRTEEN

The earl's sledge delivered Patience to St. Claire Hall before dark. With trepidation, she entered her own front door. The stark difference between her home and Beaumont Manor was evident, mostly by the lack of people, but also by the chilly foyer that greeted her.

There were no festive decorations, nor bustling staff. No warmth or light when she passed by the drawing room. The curtains were closed, probably to preserve heat, but they succeeded in making the room like a cold, dark cavern.

Continuing deeper into the silent house, Patience eventually reached the servants' quarters from which she could hear female chatter.

Pushing open the door, she encountered Eliza and Cook seated before a roaring fire, drinking tea—such a surprisingly normal and domestic scene. There was even a plate of scones between them. Cook rose immediately upon Patience's arrival, and Eliza got to her feet more slowly.

The former spoke first. "Milady, we had no word you was returning." Her wrinkled face reddened, perhaps at being caught seated and with her feet up. "We would have started a fire in the drawing room hearth and started a proper dinner."

"It is all right. Truly," Patience assured her old cook. "I didn't expect you to keep all the rooms open and heated. How could you?"

"When Lord Beaumont sent over buckets of coal," Eliza spoke up, "we thought it best to use it sparingly."

Patience hadn't known about the coal. Another generous gesture from Nathaniel. He probably had an ulterior motive, maybe so the staff didn't freeze and cease their caretaking duties or perhaps he thought they might start burning parts of the house to chase away the cold.

"You did the right thing to conserve it. How is your ankle?" Before Eliza stood, she had her leg propped on a milking stool.

"Getting better, milady. And I thank you kindly for asking. I stay off it as there's no reason to move much. But I'll be up and about again, now that you're home."

"Remain where you are," Patience said, thinking it more likely she would be joining them in their toasty domain than asking her staff to try to make the rest of the home livable.

"Where is Mr. Crawford? Lord Beaumont's footman will have brought my things in, as well as more food."

It had been galling to accept whatever charity was given, but for her staff's sake, Patience had not turned it down. Cook looked out the back window where the watery sunshine illuminated the courtyard.

"Mr. Crawford is already carrying in your trunk, milady. I'm sure he'll get everything."

"I must thank you for sending it to me. What a nice surprise to have my clothes when I finally got out of bed."

"We heard you was ever so poorly," Eliza said. Then she exchanged a glance with Cook. "But I put in evening gowns and the like, as the earl sent word you would stay there and have a Twelfth Night ball."

"Did he? Well, Lord Beaumont may throw a ball, but I will not attend." Her pride would be her only companion for the foreseeable future.

She wished she could speak to these two women with their concerned faces, but that would entirely break down the customary barrier between her and her servants. Patience could not bring her problems to them, nor let them know her closest confidences. Yet she could tell them her thoughts for what was to come.

"I am of a mind to close up the Hall and return to London as soon as the roads are passable. The townhouse will be easier to heat."

Her family's terraced home in London was modest in comparison to St. Claire Hall, yet elegantly furnished and in a safe, acceptable area. It was probably filled with dust and vermin as she hadn't resided there in nearly a year, but it could be managed with a far smaller staff.

She ought to sell it. Or the Hall. Or both.

Or marry the blasted earl and let him take all of it! But the easiest choice would bring her misery and heartache.

Without any thought, Patience sat on a velvet chair next to the hearth. A little worn, a little out of sorts, rather like herself, at one time, the crimson seat had been located in the family's side of the house.

"Tea, milady?" offered Cook as if it were the most normal thing in the world to have the lady of the house seated in the servants' parlor.

"Thank you. Yes. And then, we'll go together and see what food has been given us. Our pantry and larder shall be adequately stocked for the time being."

Glancing again at the scones, she took one without being offered and began to nibble. Her cook was skilled when she had flour, eggs, and butter.

"Delicious," Patience proclaimed, but a part of her wanted to sob. A full stomach was small consolation for an empty heart.

⌒

NATHANIEL WAS TEETERING BETWEEN melancholy and anger, between doubt and disbelief. How could he have got it so wrong? *Twice!*

A year ago, Patience allowed Lady Priscilla to destroy their burgeoning friendship. And now, inexplicably, she had told him she was not interested in him. Not at all. *Pas de tout,* as the French said.

He must have spent too much time with flirty members of the *ton,* ladies who wanted to become countesses and who fawned over him for that purpose. He had obviously lost the ability to determine a woman's true emotions. It had to be his fault because *he* was the one who had insisted she stay and had initiated each kiss.

Why, scarcely six days earlier, she had ridden off with the threat of a storm to get away from him! When he'd brought her back, after she'd recovered, he had assumed Russ was enjoying and welcomed his advances. *What a dolt!*

Nathaniel didn't tear up the marriage contract after his driver and one of his footmen took her home. Instead, he slid it into the bottom drawer of his desk, puffed out his cheeks with a sigh, and attended a highly informative dinner with his lawyer.

Later, he would drink enough brandy to feel better. For the time being, he was trying to do the same with a second glass of wine.

It was not working.

And what was he to do with the information Mr. Sudbury, his capable attorney, had discovered after

Nathaniel wrote to him on Christmas Day? The fast and drastic reduction of a family's financial estate had warranted looking into.

Despite Lady Patience not being interested in Nathaniel's assistance, he had decided to help in any case for the sake of neighborliness and knowing how his parents and hers had hosted one another. As it turned out, the St. Claire's London lawyer was taking advantage of an unsuspecting female who had been thrust into property management without any training beyond knowing how to host a party.

"The long and the short of it," Mr. Sudbury told him, "is that their solicitor, by name of Thompson, is not merely skimming off the top. He is scooping entire months' worth of revenues."

"How did you discover this?" Nathaniel asked him over dessert, which he was certain Russ would have enjoyed. She had only been gone for a day, but he couldn't help wondering what she was eating.

"The man has not been careful. He knows the lady is an orphan and thus, has boldly told the agents to send all financial statements to him. Moreover, he has moved his office and his residence this past year, as if he has experienced quite a leap in income."

"While Lady Patience freezes and starves." Anger simmered, and Nathaniel vowed he would do his utmost to fix the situation regardless of her blunt dismissal of his marriage offer.

"But we cannot accuse a man based on his buying a better house," Nathaniel pointed out.

"No," Mr. Sudbury agreed, "but we can accuse a man who keeps two sets of ledgers just in case Lady Patience asks to see her accounts."

Impressed, Nathaniel lowered his wine glass and stared at his own trusted solicitor. "How could you possibly know that?"

"Thompson has a clerk in his office who happens to be my wife's nephew. The London legal community is a small one, you see. And we are lucky that the young man puts family above employment. I promise you, I have everything I need to tap the St. Claire's lawyer on the shoulder and put him in irons. I simply need someone to ask me to press charges."

With those words, Mr. Sudbury raised an eyebrow and blinked. He was all but asking Nathaniel to be that someone.

"May *I* do so on Lady Patience's behalf?" he wondered. After all, Mr. Thompson had not personally done him any ill.

"In a shake of a lamb's tail, you could, my lord, *if* you were her husband," Mr. Sudbury explained, "or at the least, her betrothed. When shall the happy occurrence take place, by the way? I thought to meet Lady Patience during my brief stay."

Nathaniel had no intention of telling his affairs of the heart to his lawyer. "Circumstances necessitated she leave Beaumont Manor."

"Not on my account, I hope," the man said, drawing together his bushy eyebrows. "You know I conduct myself with the utmost discretion at all times."

Nathaniel had to suss out what his lawyer was saying, and then it dawned on him. "Not to worry, sir. I assure you, the lady did not go home due to fear for her reputation. Although I appreciate that you will not mention her having stayed under my roof whilst she was ill."

"Of course not. Back to the matter of Thompson my lord. What would you have me do?"

Nathaniel didn't hesitate. "Please pursue a conviction against him as soon as possible. Behave as if you are working for Lady Patience St. Claire, and I shall pay for your services."

"Very good, my lord. I shall set out in the morning and begin the proceedings. It will be a pleasure. A shady attorney blackens us all. You know what Chaucer said about one rotten apple.”

“Indeed,” Nathaniel agreed. “And you lawyers are already perceived as disreputable characters. You recall what Shakespeare said about you.”

Mr. Sudbury did not smile at that, merely looking over his spectacles with silent suffering. While he could not gainsay an earl, he didn’t have to like the insinuation. Nathaniel wished he’d kept his mouth shut rather than insulting the man who was helping him.

“Why don’t we retire to my study for some port?” Nathaniel knew his solicitor particularly enjoyed it over brandy.

On their way along the hall, Jane intercepted them.

“When will you be wanting the nine drummers, milord? We rounded up six little boys, three girls, two actual drums, and seven of cook’s pots.”

Nathaniel’s melancholy returned full force.

“Give them all a penny and send them home,” he said. “And give Cook back her pots.”

CHAPTER FOURTEEN

Patience had been home for scarcely two days, and she missed Nathaniel sorely. Thus, when Mr. Crawford found her knitting and told her someone had come from Beaumont Manor, her pulse quickened.

After some consideration, she had decided to heat the smallest drawing room, a place where she could both eat and spend her days until they left for London.

"Is it the earl?" she asked, knowing her question was foolish. Mr. Crawford would have told her at once if it were.

"No, milady, just our former maid, Jane Pearson."

"Did she walk?"

"No, milady, she came by sledge."

"How curious! Bring her to me, and—" It seemed odd to offer a servant any refreshment, but given the temperature outside, she thought she ought to. "Have Eliza or Cook bring in the tea tray."

Mr. Crawford's eyes popped at the request, but all he said was, "As you wish, milady." However, she was certain she heard him muttering about "a hurly-burly world" after he turned away, which could refer to the state of St. Claire Hall or the situation at hand with her entertaining a maid in the drawing room.

He was correct in either case!

Two minutes later, Jane with her tidily combed hair and red cheeks stood before her.

"Sit by the fire," Patience ordered.

"Oh, I couldn't sit with you, milady."

"Nonsense. Sit, or it shall be most awkward and discomforting."

Jane sat, perched on the very edge of the chair offered to her beside the hearth.

"Why have you come?" Suddenly, Patience feared something dreadful had happened. "Is everything all right?"

"No, milady. It's his lordship."

Dear God! With her heart racing, Patience asked. "Tell me at once, Jane. Is he ill?"

"Lovesick, milady. Ever since you went away, he's been blue-devilled and moping."

Lovesick! "I have only been gone a short time. How could you have noticed any change in him?"

"He didn't eat breakfast this morning, milady. That's when Mrs. Corely allowed me to borrow the sledge, with Mr. Barnes's consent, of course.

Gracious! Nathaniel's entire staff was in revolt.

"Missing a single meal is hardly a crisis. Did you ask his lordship's permission to take the sledge?"

"No, milady." The tea came in interrupting her response and making Jane's eyes bulge. "That can't be for me," she said, staring at the cook.

"If you're cold and thirsty," said Cook, "then it be for you. But don't make a habit of it. You've given young Crawford a mind to start putting on airs, too."

"I would never do that," Jane insisted, turning her stunned gaze toward Patience.

"That will be all. Thank you." Patience thought she had best regain control of the discourse. "Why don't you pour, Jane, and finish what you were saying whilst you do."

"Yes, milady." She went about the art of preparing the cups with a splash of milk and pouring the tea before adding a teaspoon of sugar to each. "I couldn't ask his lordship's permission because he would have said no." Jane said it as though Patience ought to have understood, as if *not* asking was the correct course of action.

Despite having engaged in similar deception, Patience was about to tell her what a mistake it was when the maid continued, "But we all know Lord Beaumont wants to marry you, milady. Don't you wish to marry him?"

"That is *not* your business, Jane."

"No, milady, but even us servants like to see happiness and romance. Sometimes for us, sometimes for our betters. Lord Beaumont was never so distraught as when you took to bed with the ague. We couldn't get him to eat much, nor did he sleep properly. And then he went to such trouble to bring his lawyer from London with an agreement that has all the benefit on your side."

Patience would not bother asking how the maid knew about what was being said between Nathaniel and his lawyer—the unfamiliar visitor whom she'd overheard. As a child, she had discovered that household staff knew everything.

So instead, she asked, "What kind of agreement?"

"Why, a marriage contract, milady."

"Arrogant and presuming," Patience muttered. "Beaumont wants my land and my house."

When Jane burst out laughing, Patience stared until the maid clamped a hand over her own mouth.

"My apologies, milady." Then she sipped her tea and leaned back in the chair like they were old friends. It was most disconcerting.

"What do you find so amusing? Tell me," Patience commanded.

"Excuse me, milady. I laugh because his lordship has plenty of land already. The estate in Scotland and another by the sea in Cornwall. Why would he be trying to take yours and go to the effort to marry you for it?"

The effort! "You do not know what you're talking about. I actually heard him say he wanted to take my estate under his control."

Patience pressed her lips closed, realizing she was speaking too familiarly with a maid. But Jane nodded sagely.

"Yes, milady, to make it thrive again. There's a manager who runs all the Beaumont properties. I've never seen him, but it's not merely ol' Mr. Barnes and crabby Mrs. Corely who be running things. His lordship has a manager for all his residences. Maybe more than one man. They's what keep them profitable."

She said the word as if trying it out, and Patience knew Jane had been eavesdropping at some point or been told all this by someone who had.

"Lord Beaumont wishes to make St. Claire Hall profitable," Patience said, unable to change her flat tone to one of excitement. He wouldn't do that magnanimously. He would do it once he controlled it. She sipped her tea. What Jane told her changed nothing.

"It's all in the agreement, milady," the maid insisted. "The marriage contract, as they say."

" *Who* says?"

Jane's cheeks paled slightly. "The grapevine is sacred, milady. Beaumont Manor shall go to a boy, if you're so blessed, begging your pardon for speaking of such personal things. And I don't know about them other places, but St. Claire Hall would remain yours to keep and to give to one of your children."

Well! That did change things. "Are you certain?"

The maid appeared almost affronted. "Sacred, milady, but accurate," Jane said of the servants' grapevine.

Patience knew it to be true. Leaning back, she allowed a sea of happiness to flood her. What's more, relief that Nathaniel wasn't a deceiving cad allowed the heaviness in her heart to lift. Indeed, the pain of betrayal quickly became the pang of having been cruel to the one she loved.

True, it had been a short time in one another's company, but she was already twenty-two, not a child. She knew her own mind. And she admired Nathaniel's company, his manners, his thoughts on all the many things they'd discussed. In short, he had ever shown himself to be perfect for her.

Moreover, he made her tingle from head to toe, and no other man had evoked such a strong reaction before. Otherwise, she wouldn't have let him kiss her a year earlier.

If what Jane said was true, then she had captured his affections in return, exactly as he'd told her . . . when he had asked her to marry him. *Blast her eavesdropping!*

"I believe I shall return with you and speak to Lord Beaumont, myself."

"Very good, milady." Jane picked up a biscuit and munched happily. "Let me just have a second cuppa first though, would you?"

As it turned out, with some good advice from Mr. Bellamy, the earl's driver, Patience did not return to Beaumont Manor until the following day. She'd been assured that Lord Beaumont would not know the sledge, nor Jane, was missing.

"He rides solely Bayard, milady," said the driver. "And he would be most displeased if he knew you set out for the trip after mid-day, just in case the weather turned."

"In any case," Jane said with a sigh, "his lordship canceled the pipers piping, which was probably for the best, milady. We had found two, not ten. Where were we supposed to find ten? I ask you!"

Patience made sure there was a comfortable bed for each of Nathaniel's servants. And thanks to the earl, everyone had a good meal and were kept warm.

Still, Patience had a difficult time sleeping. *What would be her reception?* She'd told Nathaniel unequivocally that she had no intention of marrying him, nor ever wished to.

Yet he was a reasonable man. Surely, he would accept her apology both for eavesdropping and for jumping to conclusions. It was not easy being a woman alone in the world. How different her life would be had her parents not set sail for Spain.

If only they had simply hopped across the English Channel like other people had done since the war with Bonaparte ended the second time? They could have enjoyed the vineyards. But no!

"I long to see groves of orange trees," her father had declared. "In Spain."

"And I cannot wait to see them with you," her mother said.

Thus, they departed from Plymouth with the intent of landing in Brest before continuing their voyage across the Bay of Biscay to Bilbao.

Naturally, her parents had invited her along, but Patience had been disinclined. She was comforted in thinking they would be pleased she had found happiness with someone they knew.

As it turned out, the earl had been correct about not traveling later in the day. Not because of inclement weather, however, but due to a lame horse. Thus, although they started out soon after breakfast, Patience and Jane had to sit under blankets with rapidly cooling bricks for longer than the ride itself when the front leg of one of the horses slid on some ice.

The animal stopped, refusing to budge or to pull the sledge another yard.

"Just like Eliza," Patience said, as Mr. Bellamy unhitched the injured horse. "I shall lead it slowly behind you," he said. "Can you drive, milady?"

"I can, indeed." She said it with great zest because she was determined to get to Nathaniel, drawn as if by a string of steel. And the tugging was growing more insistent. Even if she had to walk!

"It'll be slow going and will add an hour, I would say," Mr. Bellamy added.

Thus, their less-than merry group made its way back to Beaumont Manor.

"I should like to surprise him," Patience told them both when they arrived. Mr. Bellamy shrugged as it was no concern of his. He led the injured horse to the stable.

"I shall get Andrew to fetch your things, milady," Jane said.

"I'll slip in with you," Patience said. "I think I would like to change out of my traveling clothes."

"Yes, milady." Jane grinned conspiratorially. "Perhaps into a fancy gown."

CHAPTER FIFTEEN

Nathaniel wandered out of his study where he'd been reading the newspapers delivered from London a week earlier. Having put them aside and forgotten about them due to the excitement of having Russ in his home, he now had all the time in the world. Unfortunately, his mind kept wandering from the words on the page, and he'd given up.

Descending the stairs at a quick pace, he considered whether to go for a long ride. It would take all his effort not to direct Bayard toward the infernal lady's home.

"Do you think she has changed her mind?" he asked himself aloud, sick of his own sappy longing. "Bugger it all!"

His footsteps went toward the great room where he and Russ had such fun with the villagers on Christmas day. Or at least, he had.

The tree still stood at one end, not quite as proud and fresh as before. He would order it taken outside within the hour, as well as all the other decorations in the house. He'd thought to have his Twelfth Night guests assist in the custom of removing the greenery, but there were to be no guests.

Therefore, better a few hours early than a day late and risk poor fortune during the year, if one held with such suspicions. Although, he did not.

Wandering around the far side of the tree, regardless of good or bad luck, he merely wished to banish the poignant reminder of this worst of all Twelvetides. Getting rid of the tree was the best start.

Reaching out to snag a candied fig that had somehow escaped everyone else's eyes, Nathaniel suddenly heard singing.

"The eleventh day of Christmas,
My true love sent to me,
Eleven ladies dancing."

Russ? He circled the tree to see her standing on the other side, having come in silently on slippered feet. Wearing a gown of cranberry velvet that complimented her hair, she smiled at him, bringing sunshine to the darkest time of year. She curtseyed before coming closer.

"Ten pipers piping,
Nine drummers drumming,
Eight maids a milking,
Seven swans a swimming,
Six geese a laying,
Five gold rings."

Nathaniel closed the gap between them, fearing she was a figment of his imagination. That made more sense than thinking the lady of St. Claire Hall had magically returned to his house and was singing to him with perfect pitch.

"Four colly birds,
Three French hens,

Two turtle doves, and
A partridge in a pear tree."

Russ reached out and took his hand in hers. "I am just *one* lady, but I would be honored if you would dance with me. The mirrors at least will make it appear more like four ladies if not quite eleven."

"The honor is mine," Nathaniel returned, pulling her toward him, too close to dance. "But we have no music." And he would much rather kiss her.

Claiming her mouth, devouring her sweetness, he kissed her as if it were their last. With her, for all he knew, it was. She was mercurial and yet a solid, predictable sort of person at the same blasted time.

"*Mm,*" she purred against his mouth, and her fingers grabbed his coat, anchoring him to her.

His body burst into its own song, with his heart beating fast and his groin pulsing with desire. After many minutes, she started to push away from him.

"Russ," he protested.

"Only far enough to get into the proper position for a waltz, my lord. Can you hum a tune by Herr Schubert, for I intend to dance with you on this, the eleventh day."

Nathaniel began to hum, and they moved as one, turning and stepping, all the way down the length of the room and back, then around the tree to begin again. After doing this three times, he stopped.

"I adore dancing with you, Russ, but I must know what your appearance here means."

"It means I accept your offer of marriage. More than that. I shall be brave and tell you something and hope you forgive me. I—"

"You love me!" he declared, interrupting her. "Do you?"

"Yes, but you didn't let me say it. My gift to you, my true love, is being one of the eleven ladies dancing."

He grabbed her up high, and spun her around, faster than any waltz. Then slowly, he lowered her down the front of him until she was gazing up at him with her fierce blue gaze.

"I wanted to say it first," he said. "I think I have felt it longer. Lady Patience Russell St. Claire, I love you."

"Lord Nathaniel Beaumont, whose middle name I do not know—"

"It is James, by the way."

"Lord Nathaniel James Beaumont, I have had a stirring in my heart since last year, and it has blossomed into full-blooming love."

"It seems we got here just in time," said a female voice. Whichever servant it was, Nathaniel would dismiss her immediately for interrupting.

He turned to see a woman and a man who were not exactly strangers, familiar yet he couldn't quite place them. However, the woman in his arms gasped, going rigid.

"Unless you are married," said the man, "you had better release our daughter at once."

As their identity dawned on him, Russ collapsed in his arms.

PATIENCE OPENED HER EYES and saw the familiar blue silk canopy overhead.

"Back in bed," she muttered to herself. *Why?* Then she recalled. She must have had a relapse, perhaps been taken over by fever again due to the slow, cold journey with the lame horse. Still, the wild imaginings had seemed very real. *Cruelly so!*

She moaned and turned on her side to see her mother seated on the edge of the bed staring at her and crying.

The hallucinations continued. *Was she on the verge of expiring and shuffling off her mortal coil?*

"Mother?" she said tentatively.

"Patience!" her mother exclaimed before throwing herself across her in a full-body embrace.

"Oof!"

They stayed that way, chest to chest, and Patience had no doubt her mother was alive, for she could feel her rapid and strong heartbeat.

When finally, Lady St. Claire sat up, Patience did, too.

"I do not understand. How are you alive?"

"My dear child." Her mother put her hands on Patience's cheeks before kissing her forehead. "I have longed for this moment for nineteen months. Just to touch you and look into your eyes. I could die now satisfied to have seen you again."

"Mother, don't say that. Please tell me what happened."

"War happened, a *civil* war, they call it. I thought it anything but that. Our ship was taken, and we were caught between the Carlists and the Christinos. It was the latter who finally secured our freedom as they are supported by King William, although I have no idea if the war has ended or who shall end up in power. Nor do I care."

"This entire time, you were in Spain?"

Her mother nodded. "Under house arrest. And there weren't even any orange groves near us."

A short laugh burst from Patience, followed by a hiccup and then a flood of tears. Her mother joined in. After a minute or two, however, her mother handed her a handkerchief.

"Come along. We St. Claire women aren't known for fainting. Why, I stayed on my feet while being marched into a strange house and watched over by armed guards."

"But I thought I had lost you for so very long, my constitution is beyond shocked. You, on the other hand, knew I was alive," Patience explained.

"True." Her mother stroked her cheek again. "Let's go find your father. Naturally, he is eager to see you and hug you, too."

"Father!" Patience exclaimed and began to cry once more. "I didn't think I would have occasion to speak the word, not for my own dear father, nor lay eyes upon him ever again."

With that, she got out of bed and let her mother smooth her hair.

"He is conversing with your betrothed, if I understand the situation correctly. I always thought it would be lovely for you and our neighbor's boy to fall in love."

Patience was stunned. "You never said anything."

Her mother shrugged. "He had to get over his wild ways before he could be worthy of you. You are in love, I take it?"

"Yes, very much so."

"That's good then. But you must come home with us until the wedding. It was naughty of you to pay him a visit without a chaperone."

Patience felt like a migratory animal, one that could not seem to stay put.

"How did you find me?" she asked as they descended the stairs, arm-in-arm.

"We stopped at home, and Cook said we had just missed you."

"Then you saw the state of the house? I'm terribly sorry, Mother."

"Whatever do you mean?" Lady St. Claire sounded genuinely confounded.

"You did not notice that the fires weren't lit, nor wonder at the lack of staff to greet you?"

"Honestly, no. We were desperate to lay eyes upon you." She squeezed Patience's hand. "Everything looked the same, merely quiet and . . . I admit, a little empty. But I thought it was because you weren't there. Your father and

I really couldn't have cared less about the condition of the Hall."

They entered the drawing room, and Patience's father rose to his feet as did Nathaniel. The former opened his arms, and she ran toward him, feeling like a child again when Lord St. Claire's strong grasp enveloped her.

"Father!" she said against his chest, her tears starting to flow once more.

"Patience," her father said her name in his familiar rich, low tone, "I had feared never seeing you again." After a long moment, he drew back.

"I am so proud of you," he added. "Looking after everything by yourself. It was unconscionable of me not to make arrangements before we left. Apparently, I had a distinct lack of forethought. Can you forgive me?"

She started to shake her head. "No! I mean, yes. *I* am the one who needs forgiveness. I have let everything go to ruin. I told Mother how sorry I am."

"If I may interject," Nathaniel said.

She wished she could put her arms around him, too. Patience wanted to capture that moment in time with all those in the room. If only she could.

"A Christmas miracle," she said, keeping her gaze on the earl—*her* earl, in fact. He smiled, knowing all that was in her heart.

"Please, everyone, take a seat," he offered, then to Mr. Barnes who stood waiting, he said, "Now the ladies have joined us, please bring champagne. I believe this occasion calls for more than tea."

"Indeed," said her father. "Anything but Spanish wine, though they make a very fine sherry."

"Duly noted," Nathaniel said. "While my butler brings the finest French bubbles, I must tell you how presumptuous I have been, yet I believe you will forgive me."

To Patience's amazement, and adding to the already astonishing proceedings of the day, she learned that her father's attorney had been stealing from her practically since the moment of her parents' purported death. Nathaniel's own attorney was setting things to rights.

"Then I am not a failure," Patience said, from her seat between her parents. She squirmed, unable to contain her excitement over her parents being among the living. "Nor was I overspending."

"You did very well with all you had to handle," her mother said.

Her father leaned forward, resting an elbow on his knee. "Now, Lord Beaumont, before we let champagne go to our heads, let's discuss the marriage contract."

Her fine-looking earl nodded somberly, but then he winked at Patience. Suddenly, she recalled something tremendous and couldn't help a burst of joyful laughter.

"Father," she said, when she could speak, "do you know Lord Beaumont has an orangery? Isn't that a remarkable coincidence? Why, you didn't have to go to Spain at all."

EPILOGUE

Ramsden Heath, England, 1836

"One more dance, Lady Beaumont?" Nathaniel asked his wife a year later. "And then I shall whisk you away to our bed."

"Gladly," Russ said. He marveled at her glowing beauty, her cheeks particularly rosy, and her red hair shining in the candlelight, set off perfectly by her sapphire-blue gown.

The musicians began a waltz, as he had instructed for the final dance. Many of their overnight guests had already retired to their rooms, including his mother, his sister, and her family. Some not-too-distant neighbors had left, including Lady Kepelton. A few lingering merrymakers decided to sit out the last dance, resting on chairs, sipping the dregs of their champagne.

Among these was Lady Terrence, previously Lady Priscilla Malcolm Price. She had caught herself a baron during the high season, poor sap. Upon learning of his and Russ's nuptials, the chit had written to his new countess to apologize and confess her perfidy. Since finding true love, the lady had been ever so ashamed at having nearly ruined another's happiness.

Russ, being Russ, had forgiven and invited Lord and Lady Terrence to the Twelfth Night ball. In fact, the baron wasn't a bad chap at all, even if Nathaniel mistrusted the man's taste in women.

His wife's parents approached the dance floor, and Russ's smile widened as the four of them, with a few other determined souls, took a last twirl around the great room.

With one hand resting on the small of Russ's back and the other holding her delicate hand, Nathaniel knew utter happiness. Every day was a blessing, and every night was a thrilling dance of another kind.

He could not have anticipated their marriage being so satisfying, nor so uncomplicated. Moreover, he enjoyed convincing her at every turn that he was an entirely reformed man, one who would never again desire another female apart from her.

And why would he? His red-headed lady was now his best friend and an excellent lover. Living with her was the most fun he had ever had, although twelve days earlier, on Christmas day, she had again beaten him at Snap Dragon!

EXHAUSTED FROM DAYS OF preparation and then the festive gathering, Patience was happy to retire to the bedroom she shared with her husband at the conclusion of their Twelfth Night ball. Since the clock had struck midnight two hours earlier, it was already the sixth of January, officially the twelfth day of Christmas, a seemingly topsy-turvy backward sequence in which the twelfth night preceded the day.

As a child, it had confused her, but she knew when she awakened in a few hours, the Twelvetide would be drawing to a close.

Her beloved parents were spending the night, just as they had done twelve months earlier after arriving like impossible phantoms. After discovering Nathaniel's marriage contract was generous and that their own home was lacking most everything including staff, they had remained at Beaumont Manor and let Patience sleep under the same roof as her fiancé.

A week later, after beginning to remedy the issues at St. Claire Hall, the three of them had moved back into their home where she stayed until her spring wedding.

Now, in the green-and-gold bedchamber, formerly the earl's alone, Patience sagged against Nathaniel while they hugged one another, standing before the warm coals in the hearth. With her husband beginning to pull the pins from her hair, tossing them hither and yon, she rested in his embrace, her cheek on his chest.

"I am glad our child won't be a Christmas baby," she said, feeling confident at three months along that she would carry him or her until the birth. "It would be a gluttony of blessings, when we already have so much to be thankful for this time of year."

Some days, she had to stop and pinch herself, scarcely believing she was not an orphan and that her parents would be grandparents. Moreover, she was no longer an only child after growing a fond attachment to Nathaniel's sister, who promised to tell her any tips and tricks of new motherhood.

Happily, her mother-in-law had welcomed Patience warmly into the family, pleased to see her son settle down and carry on the earldom by starting a family. Moreover, the Dowager Countess had decided to move in permanently with her daughter to give the newlyweds space to enjoy their marriage.

Enjoy it, they did! Almost nightly and sometimes during the day, too.

As Nathaniel ran his fingers through her hair and then kneaded her back, she wished she felt renewed vigor. Alas, his ministrations were relaxing her further toward sleep.

"Mm," she sighed. "Undress me, please, and I shall . . . well, I will lie on the bed and watch you remove your own clothing for I am too tired to do aught else."

He laughed. "I will happily play your lady's maid. And hold you in my arms, expecting nothing but to hear your gentle snores—even though my pole shall be like a sturdy oak branch, jutting forth."

Patience giggled at the image. She let him spin her to face away from him before he undid the fancy ribbons of her ballgown. He slid it off her, and then sent her petticoat falling past her hips to the carpet.

Yawning, she stretched, and then began to undo her own corset before he shoved her slow, fumbling fingers aside and finished for her.

"There," he said, "to bed," and he gave her bottom a swift smack.

But she went instead toward the nightstand where Jane, now her permanent lady's maid, always left a jug of water, soap, and tooth powders. Eliza had stayed behind at the Hall to be with Mr. Crawford and serve Lord and Lady St. Claire as always.

"*Ugh!*" Patience groaned. "Sometimes, when my eyelids feel so heavy, I don't want to do this, but then I think of teaching cleanliness to our child, and I know I must."

She washed her face and brushed her teeth before climbing into bed with a sigh. Nate used the soap, then scrubbed his teeth, before undressing, which Patience enjoyed watching more than any play or concert in London.

"You are the most handsome naked man I have ever seen," she declared.

"Am I not the *only* naked man you have ever seen?" he asked, climbing into bed beside her.

"In the flesh? Yes. But I've seen paintings and statues. You are far superior to any of them."

Drawing the covers over them, he turned on his side, gathering her close. until her back side was snugged to his front.

"None of them had your *pole* either," she said, "if my memory serves me."

When he laughed, she felt his arousal move against her, and despite the late hour, Patience's own desire flickered into flames. She pressed against him as his arms tightened around her.

"The twelfth day of Christmas, my true love sent to me twelve leaping lords," she whispered.

"Russ, what are you saying? Shall I leap atop you and show you how much I love you?"

"Yes, my lord. I think it best if you do. Not twelve times, though. But once, and I shall sleep more soundly for it."

Gently, he rolled her onto her back. "I shall play Snap Dragon, I think. I'll use my lapping tongue and feast upon your plums."

He took her nipple into his mouth, dampening the thin linen of her shift. She smiled at his playful manner, while a frisson of excitement danced through her, wakening her body further.

Sinking her fingers into his soft, dark hair, a luxury she never tired of, Patience told him, "Then tonight, my lord, I shall let *you* win the game. And gladly."

Finis

ABOUT THE AUTHOR

USA Today bestselling author Sydney Jane Baily writes historical romance with happily-ever-after stories, engaging characters and attention to period detail.

Born and raised in California, she has traveled the world, spending a lot of exceedingly happy time in the U.K. where her extended family resides, eating fish and chips, drinking shandies, and snacking on Maltesers and Cadbury bars. Sydney currently lives in New England with her family—human, canine, and feline.

You can learn more about her books, read her blog, sign up for her newsletter (and get a free book), and contact her via her website at SydneyJaneBaily.com. She loves to hear from her readers.